OMEGA GROWN

BOOK SEVEN OF THE NORTHERN LODGE PACK SERIES

SUSI HAWKE

AN M/PREG PARANORMAL ROMANCE

Cover Art Designed by Cosmic Letterz

What happens when your fated mate is also your natural predator?

Join my mailing list and get your FREE copy of The Rabbit Chase:

https://dl.bookfunnel.com/vfk1sa9pu3

Twitter:
https://twitter.com/SusiHawkeAuthor

Facebook:
https://www.facebook.com/SusiHawkeAuthor

ALSO BY SUSI HAWKE

Northern Lodge Pack Series

Omega Stolen: Book 1

Omega Remembered: Book 2

Omega Healed: Book 3

Omega Shared: Book 4

Omega Matured: Book 5

Omega Accepted: Book 6

Omega Grown: Book 7

Northern Pines Den Series

Alpha's Heart: Book 1

Alpha's Mates: Book 2

Alpha's Strength: Book 3

Alpha's Wolf: Book 4

Alpha's Redemption: Book 5

Alpha's Solstice: Book 6

Blood Legacy Chronicles

Alpha's Dream: Book 1

Non-Shifter Contemporary Mpreg

Pumpkin Spiced Omega: The Hollydale Omegas - Book 1

Cinnamon Spiced Omega: The Hollydale Omegas - Book 2

Peppermint Spiced Omega: The Hollydale Omegas - Book 3

This book is lovingly dedicated to all of the fantastic readers that have encouraged and supported me as a new author. The Facebook & Twitter "likes", "follows" and private messages, the public posts and "shares", and your emails have all meant so much more to me than you'll ever know. Putting oneself out there for open critique is a scary, scary thing but you've all made me feel so very welcome in the mpreg world. This isn't the end of the guys from the Northern Lodge Pack, but moving forward we will focus less on them and more on new characters and settings... such as the friendly bears in the neighboring den. You'll understand more once you've read this final chapter. Keep an eye on my newsletter for upcoming books that relate to this series, and my other works.

Thank you for reading my books!
- Susi

CHAPTER 1

RYAN

The look on the pack's face when the new omega walked in was priceless. He was one of a couple dozen new members that had just been vetted to join our pack here at the lodge. While everyone else stared at him with a mix of awe, shock, humor, and in some cases, horror, I looked at him and saw a friend.

As soon as Alpha Jake ended the welcome meeting, I made my way over to him. He was a little twink of a thing, just like me. It was going to be awesome to have another tiny unclaimed omega in the pack.

His hair was nothing short of legendary. Cut in a faux-hawk that was uber short on the sides and longer on top, he'd spiked it up into gelled points that ran across the top of his head and down the back. And the color! It was dyed a pale, cotton candy blue.

His ears had big holes in them, with some sort of ring

lining the inside edge of the hole. His clothes, in contrast, were pretty tame. He wore a pair of black skinny jeans and a red tank that had been cropped short enough that his chiseled abs flashed with every movement. His pink punk boots with the bright yellow laces were epic.

I noticed him giving me the once-over as I approached. I grinned and gave him the same eye treatment right back. He was laughing when I walked up with a smirk on my face. He might be cool as fuck, but this was my pack. No way was I gonna let myself be intimidated by the new kid.

"Hey, there," I said with the cockiest tone I could muster. "I'm Ryan. Welcome."

He nodded. "I'm Taylor. Nice to meet ya. Anything to do around here?"

I grimaced, and glanced around to see if anyone was paying attention. "Not really. Have you been upstairs to the dorms to pick a room yet?"

"Hell no. I think my cousin is hoping to have me room with him, but he's boring as fuck. Why? You need a roomie?" He tilted his hip and planted a hand there as he struck a pose. I was short, but this kid was half a head shorter than me. And yet, he managed to pull off looking taller with all the attitude he was packing in that tiny ass twink body.

"I wasn't in the market for one. I just got rid of my brother last year when he got mated. But, I dunno. You might be okay if you wanna hang." I looked around to see if my brother was paying attention to what I was doing. "Come on, I'll take you up. We'll see about rooming together, if you want."

I weaved through the crowd of people with Taylor right behind me. We almost made it to the stairs when Luke stepped in front of me with my niece, Daisy, on his hip. His mate, Daniel, was naturally right there beside him, holding the other two of their triplets.

"Hey, Ryan," Luke chirped in a saccharine voice. "Leaving so soon? Weren't you going to introduce your big brother to your new friend?"

I gritted my teeth and resisted the urge to roll my eyes. Fucking Luke. I loved the hell out of my brother—he'd always been there for me, even when our lives were at the shittiest points. But Fenris above knew that he was the bossiest little omega on earth. He always acted like he was my parent, and not just a couple of years older than me. And since his mate was the second-in-command to our pack Alpha, he had the heat to back him up when he tried to control my life.

"I wasn't leaving. I was taking Taylor up to help him find a room in the dorms." I turned to include Taylor. He stepped up beside me with an angelic smile. "Taylor, this is my brother, Luke. The big guy beside him is his mate, Daniel. The little pipsqueaks are my niece, Daisy, and her two brothers, Zeke and Zander."

I waved a hand in Taylor's direction. "Luke, Daniel, this is Taylor. Obviously, he's one of the new omegas."

Zeke was reaching for me, trying to wriggle out of his dad's firm hold. Luke turned to Taylor and said, "Well, it's nice to meet you, Taylor. I hope you'll feel welcome here." He turned to me and said, "Are you coming by later? The pups miss you."

Translation: Luke wanted me to come babysit so that he could have alone time with Daniel. Luke pointedly glanced at Zeke, who was babbling excitedly in his mission to get to me. I leaned over and kissed the top of Zeke's head but skirted back quickly before one of his chubby little hands could catch me.

"Sorry, but I can't tonight. I promised Taylor I'd help him settle in. You know, like Daniel and Alpha Jake just asked us to do in the meeting? To make our new pack-mates feel welcome? Anyway, I'll try and come by in the next day or two."

Taylor helpfully added, "Yeah, it was super sweet of Ryan to offer to help me get settled in here. I mean, my look is super cool back home but I don't exactly fit in here from what I see. It was awesome to make a non-judgmental friend on my first day."

Luke's eyes narrowed, yet his smile never wavered. Daniel looked at me with a knowing smirk as he commented dryly to Taylor, "Well, it's a good thing that your alpha brother and omega cousin both came here too,

Taylor. We'd hate to see you only have Ryan for a support system. Life changes can be rough."

Before anything else could be said, my main man Zander started crying. Loud. Like super loud. His little face was bright red as he shrieked angrily. "Wow, I better let you guys get the Trips home. It sounds like Zander needs his daddies and I really need to get going anyway."

I smiled jauntily and headed up the stairs. Taylor said a polite goodbye and followed me up. We made it up to the third floor where the single dorms were located without running into anyone else. I pointed things out to Taylor as I led him to my room.

"That side is alpha rooms only, we're on the other side of the hall. There's an unofficial understanding that we each stay on our own sides of the hall. Each side has its own communal bathrooms." I pointed them out as we passed by. "There's several showers, sinks, and toilets in each so you usually don't have to wait. Well, that might be different now that there's so many of you joining us. But there's a lot of room up here."

I opened my door and flipped on the light. "My room used to belong to the last omega that got mated. He's huge 'cuz he's a bear shifter, that's why there's the one big bed in here. I snapped it up when he moved out."

"Damn. I was actually hoping we could room together, but I doubt you'd want to share a bed." Taylor said this as he looked around my room.

"I mean, we could always drag a single in from another room? I don't wanna share a bed though. I did that enough growing up with my brother. But there's plenty of room over there for a bed." I pointed to the opposite corner of the room. "There used to be another bed in here, but they moved it out when Oskar's bed was brought in."

I glanced over at Taylor speculatively. "I kinda like the idea of rooming with you, though. And not just because I think it will make Luke shit a brick."

Taylor snorted. "Yeah, I kinda get that a lot. People expect me to be trouble when they see me coming. Judgmental assholes."

I nodded. "I get that. Well, I do tend to get in trouble, that's why my brother is always trying to boss me around. Which just makes me want to fuck with him more." I shrugged. "It's a vicious cycle, I guess."

Taylor smirked. "Or just brothers being brothers. I've always screwed with my brother too. It's too easy. You'll see when you meet him. Just don't try to hook up with him or anything, that would be weird."

I gulped. "I've, umm, never exactly done that yet anyway."

Taylor's eyebrows shot up. "How old are you?"

"I'm nineteen, almost twenty. But, you gotta understand. This is a small pack, and I was super young when I came here. The alphas were all grown, and I was like the kid brother to everyone. Your group is the first chance that I've ever had to check out alphas that didn't feel like family. Well, there's the local bears, but I haven't spent much time around them. And the ones that have come around got snapped right up by their true-mates."

"Yeah, I heard that you guys have a lot of fated matings up here. Now, tell me more about the bears! I wanna see one! I bet they're huge, right?" Taylor looked excited about the idea.

"Oh, yeah. Well, there's one single bear alpha here, but I haven't talked to him yet. He teaches in the schoolhouse. He also lives there, so he doesn't come around much."

Taylor looked at me and grinned. "Then he's the first one that we're checking out! But first, do you wanna go and see about finding me a bed or should I just sleep with you for tonight?" He looked me up and down again. "If you want, I can even teach you a few things. You're not my type; I'm totally into alphas. But I'd be happy to show you a few things."

I gulped. "Umm. I don't wanna sound like a total hick, but do omegas really do stuff like that together?"

Taylor shrugged. "I don't know if all of them do, but me personally? I like to get off and I'm not too picky about who I do it with if I'm horny enough. Like I said, I can show you a few things. I mean, it's not like we can get each other pregnant, right?"

"But what about our future mates? Wouldn't they be pissed that we didn't wait for them instead?" I hated to sound like a kid, but I worried about shit like that.

Taylor walked over and stood in front of me. He looked at me studiously for a minute then grabbed my hips and jerked me against him. I swallowed nervously when I felt a hard dick push up against me. He smirked, then leaned over and kissed me!

After a second, I started kissing him back. It was weird. It was cool. It was such a terrifying turn-on. Taylor's tongue pushed through my lips, and I tilted my head to kiss him more. My dick got so hard, I thought it would break off if anything touched it. Then Taylor did. He reached down and grabbed me through my jeans.

His hand cupped my crotch, while he pushed against my hard dick with the base of his palm. He broke the kiss and pulled away suddenly. Dropping his hands, he stepped back and cupped his own crotch while he leered at me with a knowing smirk. "It's up to you, Ryan. You can worry about pissing off your unknown future alpha, or you can be fuck-buddies with me. I'm good either way. We can be friends, we can be fuck-buddies, or we can be both. I'm down with whatever."

I nodded jerkily, licking the taste of him from my lips as I reached down and readjusted my junk. "O-okay. I'll think about it. But yeah, you can totally spend the night with me until we find you a bed."

Taylor winked and headed for the door. "Cool. Come back downstairs with me and help me get my stuff from the van then, roomie."

I followed him, wondering what the hell I'd just gotten myself into, and if I really wanted to find a way out. Whatever I did or didn't decide to do with him, I knew already that I wanted to spend a lot more time with Taylor.

CHAPTER 2

IVAN

The two young wolf omegas walked past me, and I could smell the arousal on both of them. I watched them curiously. The tiny one looked like a peacock with that ridiculous hair and the way he flounced along when he walked. The other one, Ryan, was following him like an eager little puppy dog.

I chuckled to myself as I realized what an apt description it was to compare the young wolf to a puppy dog. Following them, I stepped out onto the wide porch and took a seat on the railing at the far end where I merged with the shadows.

They appeared to be getting the peacock's bags from one of the vans that the new pack members had driven up here. I wondered what they'd been up to, for them both to be smelling like sex and for Ryan to have that guilty look on his face.

I'd been watching Ryan from afar for the past few months. I hadn't gotten close enough to scent him yet, let alone speak to him, but my bear was intrigued by the boy. So far I'd been holding off from getting closer. I was cautious in my personal life. I had to be, as I was a teacher. One who was entrusted with educating young minds needed to be an good example at all times, and live a life above reproach.

Somehow, I didn't think dating a boy a decade my junior would make me look like a pillar of our small community. Especially a beloved brat like Ryan. No, nothing short of confirming that he was my mate would make me take that risk. And he was definitely a brat. I'd watched him pout and cajole to get his way with the other alphas in the pack. They all treated him like a pampered baby brother.

The only ones that seemed immune to his charms were his brother, Luke, and Daniel, Luke's mate. Aside from my bear's interest, the other reason that I still gave him consideration was my father. Ryan was currently working in the clinic for Dad. He'd been running the office efficiently for several months now. Dad had nothing but praise for the boy. My father's opinion held a lot of weight with me. He was a reasonable man who had always been a fine judge of character.

It concerned me now, this friendship that Ryan appeared to have struck up with the peacock. That sex scent could only mean that they'd been fooling around. I'd never heard of omegas doing that together, but it didn't surprise me. They were a couple of young, healthy guys after all. No, I didn't care about omegas fooling around in general. I did care though, that the peacock was touching Ryan.

I grunted. I didn't have a right to get involved. Especially when I didn't know if he was even my mate. All I knew was that my bear was awfully intrigued by him. I watched then, as Ryan dropped the bag he held. When he bent to retrieve it, the peacock reached out and grabbed Ryan's perky buttock.

I bit back a growl and shoved my bear back into place. I needed more information, dammit. And yet, it didn't look as though I had time left to dally. The peacock would do more than grab his butt once they were alone upstairs under the cover of darkness, I knew that much just from watching him.

I stood and walked back over to lean against the railing by the stairs. The boys were coming up the walk now. When Ryan took another step closer, I smelled it in one burst of deliciousness. He smelled like a crisp, fresh bite of tart pear. Peacock stepped a little closer, swinging his arm around Ryan's shoulder and joking about a sleep-over or some such nonsense.

"What are you boys up to out here?" I asked, amused how they both jerked when I startled them. "Silly me, I thought that I would be alone out here." Okay, I was lying. But all is fair in love and war.

Peacock stepped away from Ryan, obviously not wanting

to be seen flirting with the other omega. My omega. Even if he didn't know it yet. Ryan looked up at me and smiled nervously.

"Uh. Hi, there. You're Ivan, right?" His eyes told me that he knew exactly who I was, but I nodded back in agreement. He turned to the peacock and explained. "This is Ivan. He's the bear alpha that teaches the pups. I work for his dad."

Ryan turned back to me. "This is Taylor. He's one of the new pack members that just arrived. I'm showing him around. He's going to be my new roommate."

Thankfully, Daniel came walking up right then before I could respond. "Actually, boys, I'm afraid that there's been a misunderstanding. I've already assigned rooms to everyone, I'm sorry. It dawned on me after I left that you guys had mentioned taking Taylor up to pick out a room when we were talking earlier."

Ryan's plush bottom lip jutted out into a pout as he turned mutinous eyes onto Daniel. "I'm sorry, Daniel. But can I just ask if you remembered this before or after my brother discussed it with you?"

Like I thought, Daniel didn't fall for Ryan's bratty crap. "Ryan, what I discuss with your brother is our business. And although I don't need to explain myself to pack members, I will tell you anyway. We didn't need to assign rooms in the dorms in the past, because there was at least double the amount of beds and space than our small pack required. The cabins and family rooms have been more of an issue in that department."

Daniel nodded over at me, including me in the conversation. "With so many new members, it was important to assign rooms and to avoid any possible problems. I meant to go over it in the meeting, but we got distracted. Kai is inside directing everyone to their assigned rooms right now."

He turned to Taylor and explained, "Taylor, Kai is first-mate of our pack, mated to the Alpha. Come in with me, and I'll introduce you so that he can help you get settled. I chose roommates based on your different backgrounds and personalities. I have you in with your cousin, and two brothers that rode in the other van. They're twins. I don't know if you met them?"

Taylor sneered before quickly schooling his face into a fake smile as he replied. "I saw them earlier. We haven't had the pleasure of meeting just yet. And, forgive me if I offend you, but what exactly about my personality was it that made you think that I would belong with my lame ass cousin and the juicy-fruit twins?"

Daniel's eyes looked thunderous as he replied. "To be frank? I think that they will be a steadying influence on you, young man. And as for your cousin? Your brother insisted on it. He explained that your cousin is alone in the world now that his mate has passed away. So you can choose to get along with them, or you can be miserable. Either way, the Alpha and I expect your cooperation.

And Taylor? It would go a long way with us if you would be kind to your cousin. He's had a hard go of it this past year from what I was told."

Ryan wisely kept his mouth shut; instead he stood there quietly looking down at the ground while Daniel dealt with the peacock. I wondered even more about Ryan. It seemed as if the brat knew how to behave when the situation called for it. He also seemed submissive to authority figures. Interesting.

Peacock turned to Ryan and clapped him on the shoulder with a false bravado. "Well, we were almost roomies! That's cool though, right? We'll just have to hang out another time. I mean, it's not like we won't be on the same floor anyway. I guess I need to go with your brother's mate now and meet this Kai person."

Ryan smiled at his new buddy. "Kai is cool. You'll like him. I'll pop by later and say good-night so that I can meet your cousin." His eyes darkened, as if remembering bad experiences. "I hate to think of how alone he must be feeling. It's good that you can be there for him, Taylor."

Peacock puffed up a little at that. Daniel jerked his chin toward him and said, "Okay, let's go in then. Kai needs to put his pups to bed soon, I think Jake said." As he walked past Ryan, Daniel stopped to rest a calming hand on his neck for a moment.

"Ryan, I know that you think Luke is heavy-handed. It's rough, I'm sure, because he's not much older than you.

But remember that your brother loves you. He just wants to see you safe and happy after all you two went through as pups. Be patient with him, kid. He means well."

Ryan nodded jerkily. I could see the frustration in his stiff shoulders and clenched jaw. Daniel squeezed his neck and sent a wave of calm over Ryan. The scent of the alpha pheromones were easily detected. Ryan's lips pinched tighter as he resisted, but he did seem to relax a notch or two.

"Thanks, Daniel. I'll try and keep that in mind. Just, umm," he sighed and shook his head before he continued. "Could you just tell him that he's the Trips' dad, not mine? I need a brother, not a father."

Daniel nodded with a slight frown, and took the peacock's bag from Ryan's hand before he moved on to where the kid was waiting at the foot of the stairs. Ryan waited until they went inside, then looked up at me. "I'm sorry that you had to hear all that the first time that we actually met each other."

I smiled gently at him and jerked my chin toward the porch benches that hugged the wall of the house. "Why don't you sit down and tell me about it? I'm a good listener, or so I've been told."

Ryan looked reluctantly intrigued by me as he climbed the steps. When Ryan stepped up beside me, he froze. His pupils dilated and nostrils flared as he took a long, inhaled sniff of me. I quirked a brow and looked down at him with a knowing smirk. His head didn't quite reach my shoulder, as he stood beside me. Small and slim, he was a short little drink of water.

"What's wrong, my boy?" I asked softly. "Do you smell something good?"

His head jerked to glance around before he finally peered up at me. Ryan looked at me in confusion. "Is that smell coming from you?"

I shrugged and put my hand on the small of his back while I guided him over to a bench at the far end of the porch. "I wouldn't know, Ryan. First you'd have to tell me what it is that you're smelling."

Ryan sat down at the far end of the bench. Although there was plenty of room, I sat down beside him. I was crowding him, sitting so close that I could feel the heat from his leg where it pressed against mine. I reached my arm out behind the boy, stretching it across the back of the bench.

Ryan tilted his head up at an angle, looking me over through the side of his luminous brown eyes. Although we sat in the shadows, there was enough moonlight to see each other clearly. He smirked and bravely sat taller.

"Just because you smell good to my wolf doesn't mean that I'm in the market for a mate. I figured that I should probably let you know that, Ivan. And all this," he paused and waved a hand up and down to demonstrate my large alpha body. "All this alpha authority shit doesn't work for me. So don't think you're going to be tying me down and making babies with me anytime soon. You don't know me. Just because some arcane god like Fenris has decided that we were fated to be together doesn't mean that I'm going to jump on your knot simply because my wolf apparently has decided that he likes the smell of pineapple."

My lips tilted up to one side. Damn, this boy was a fire-cracker! I looked down at him with thinly veiled amusement. "Pineapple, huh? And you think that you know all about me and my intentions just by looking at me? Wow, you must be pretty observant for a boy at the ripe old age of, what, nineteen? Twenty? Boy, I was living on my own among the humans, working two jobs and going to college full-time at your age. All this *alpha shit* you see isn't because I'm an alpha. It's because I'm a grown ass man that's made my own way in the world by working hard to achieve my goals and not bullshitting around while I did it."

Ryan crossed his arms and glared at me. "Just because I'm young doesn't mean that I don't know how to read people. I wouldn't have survived to adulthood without knowing how read the intentions of others, especially fucking alphas looking for a hole to dip their wick in."

"Damn, Ryan! You've got a hell of a mouth on you for such a sweet looking omega boy." I bit back a laugh. I was delighted by this boy, I just didn't want to show my cards yet. "Now, listen. I don't know what you think that you've been through in your short life, but I know from my dad that you've lived here since before you had hair on your balls. And I can sure as hell tell by the way the wolf alphas around here coddle you that you haven't had much hardship since you've been here."

Ryan surprised me when his shoulders slumped instead of biting back at me. He shook his head as he looked down at his lap. "Yeah. That's true, I guess. But riddle me this, Ivan. How many years of coddling will it take to do away with the nightmares I still have from the things that happened in the first two-thirds of my life? Hmm? Tell me, *alpha*, because I'd really like to know."

I felt like shit now. I'd been enjoying our banter, but I hadn't realized that my carelessly spoken words would score a direct hit. The snarky way that he'd called me alpha would have told me that much, even if his body language hadn't.

"Ryan, please allow me to apologize. You're right. I don't know you, or what you've experienced in your young life. Hell, maybe there's a good reason why the alphas around here let you wrap them around your little finger. But realize this, you don't know me either. I had good intentions when I invited you to talk. The fact that we caught each other's scents was unexpected."

I stopped, and let out a sigh. "Okay. Let me back up. I had a feeling that there was a possibility that we could find ourselves to be mates if we got close enough. But that was only because my bear has been noticing you and showing interest. I didn't know for sure until I smelled you just now. And then you smelled me, and now here we are. Can we maybe just go back a few minutes and start fresh?"

Ryan looked up at me with a soft smile. "I'd like that. And, I don't like that you think I'm a brat." He looked down at his lap, fiddling with a fingernail. "I guess I am sometimes, but that's because that's all anyone expects of me and old habits die hard." He groaned and threw his head back against my arm as he looked up into the dark shadows overhead. "That sounds like a fucking cop-out. And maybe it is. But I'm so sick of only being Luke's kid brother that always needs looking after."

He feigned a high-pitched voice and said, "Oh, *poor* Ryan! He was bought as a pup by an *evil* alpha who wanted to make him a *sex*-slave. Let's give him ice-cream and *never* take him seriously for the rest of his life!"

His voice dropped back to normal as he continued. "You wanna know why the alphas all coddle me? Ask them to tell you about why we came here and formed the pack. And no, I'm not telling you this to gain your sympathy. If anything, I like the fact that you're not trying to baby and coddle me. It actually makes me respect you a little. Just don't push it. And I'm still not ready to get tied down. Just putting that out there right now."

I smiled to myself, thinking how very much I would love to baby him. But not yet. He didn't need that right now. Ryan needed someone who would call him on his shit and be a strong man that he could to trust enough to lean on. Someone dominant without being an abusive ass.

I could be all of that for him. I could show him that being submissive to his alpha wouldn't make him weak. In fact, it was quite the opposite. We would balance each other. Eventually. But first I had to earn his trust. And as he had so aptly said, he would respect me more if I didn't coddle him.

"Did I put you to sleep over there? You went quiet on me," Ryan said as he turned his head and looked up at me with that trademark pout.

I reached up and ran a finger over that lower lip that was stuck out so invitingly. "Not at all, my boy. I was actually thinking about how you keep mentioning get tied down by me. That was twice now, wasn't it? Do you have a little fantasy life that I should know about, Ryan?" I winked lasciviously and licked my lips, chuckling as he squirmed.

"Don't be gross, old man. You know what I meant." Ryan's head still leaned against my arm, and the gleam in his eye told me that he wasn't as disinterested as he would have me believe.

"Speaking of fantasies. Is there anything I should know about you and that little peacock kid that you were with earlier?" I gently curled my arm that was under his head and rested my hand on his slender shoulder.

He didn't move out of my partial embrace, but his eyes flared with a hint of heat as he spoke. "Peacock kid? Do you mean Taylor? I really don't think that's any of your business, Ivan. Let's just say that he's a friend, and leave it at that."

"Friends don't grab each other's asses, my boy. At least, none of the friends that I've known anyway." I kept my voice calm, but needed him to hear my displeasure. "Not to mention the fact that you reek of him, even now."

"Like I said, I really don't think it's any of your business. I'll acknowledge that we're fated, but we're not mates." His voice was edging into petulance again.

His voice grew silky as he said, "You know what? Maybe we're going about this the wrong way. I mean, I have no problem being fuck-buddies until I'm ready to get mated someday. Maybe you can show me a few things. I mean, you *are* a teacher."

I jerked my arm back as I sat up and looked at him in horror. "Fuck-buddies? What the hell kind of shit are you talking about? I would never disrespect you or any other omega by fucking around like that without the security of a claim! And I know that you didn't learn that from anyone here. Where the hell did you pick that up?"

I could easily smell Ryan's embarrassment, yet he refused to let it show on his face. Little brat. *Fuck-buddies?* Ryan stood up and braced his hands on his slim hips as he glared down at me. Even though I was seated, he barely towered over me.

"I hear things," he said in his brat voice, obviously

working himself up into full tantrum mode. "I'm not a complete idiot, you know. And I don't like it when you judge me! First you question me about my private friendship with Taylor, and snark about him touching my ass. Now you want to act like I'm a dirty boy because I offered to fuck you without a claim? I don't need to be lectured, judged, or bossed around, *Daddy*."

His tantrum was having the unintended effect of turning me on for some weird reason. And when he called me *Daddy* like that? *Fuck me*. My dick twitched and began to show a little interest in the proceedings. I looked up at Ryan and gave him a slow wink.

"Call me Daddy like that again, my boy. Maybe if you do then Daddy will show you how much he would like to turn his little brat over Daddy's knees. Go ahead, Ryan. I dare you."

Ryan stamped his foot and growled at me. He actually growled! It was so adorable that I wanted to yank him down on my lap. Then I would show him a thing or two about why riling up an alpha wasn't the best plan if he didn't want to get claimed and mated.

Calmly, I raised a brow and asked, "Are you done with your little fit now, brat? Or should I give you another minute?"

"Aargh! I'm done with this shit! I'll talk to you when you want to treat me like an adult. Until then, I'm going to my room!" He started to stalk away.

"Go ahead, my boy. Send yourself to your room, that's where little brats need to go when they misbehave anyway. Oh, and Ryan? If you want me to treat you like an adult? You should maybe try acting like one."

Ryan stomped off and went inside, slamming the door behind him. I grinned and leaned back with my hands behind my head. Oh, yeah. This was gonna be fun. I had to wonder how long my boy would fume before he came back to poke at me again for a reaction. I already was getting to know him well enough to know one thing. There was no way in hell that he wasn't going to show up at my door in full brat mode to tell me off. It was just a matter of how long it would take him to do it.

The screen door creaked open, and Daniel stepped out. He looked around, and then came over when he saw me sitting there. He sat down on the next bench over, and leaned back. We sat there in a companionable silence for a bit. Then he looked over at me and said, "So. My mate's kid brother sure was in a huff when he came inside. He went upstairs cussing a blue streak and muttering about Ivan the alpha-hole. Anything I need to know about here? Or should I just stay out of it?"

I looked over at him curiously. "Well, damn. You don't sound overly concerned."

Daniel shook his head and flapped his hand in a derisive wave. "That's because I'm not. Ryan's a spoiled little shit. My mate worries about him all the time. Luke tries to help him, but nothing changes with that kid. It pisses me off. I don't mean to sound like an asshole, but it's getting old. I think maybe it's just past time that Ryan grew up."

Even though I knew Daniel to be a kind, logical, and fair-minded man, it was more than a little obvious that he was viewing Ryan through Luke's eyes. And reacting to his mate's worries, no doubt. But Ryan was my mate, and Daniel's words were raising my hackles. I wasn't about to let anyone talk shit about my boy, whether it was based in fact or not.

"Perhaps he would grow up a little faster if his brother would let him, Daniel." I held up a hand as Daniel sat up with a glare. "Hold on, I'm not saying that Luke doesn't have a right to worry. Or even that you don't have the right to get upset on your mate's behalf. But Ryan is more than just a spoiled brat. I'm starting to think that maybe you guys don't know him as well as you think you do."

"Ivan, I'm going to refrain from reacting to that statement, if for no other reason than because of the utmost respect that I hold for both you and your father. But I'm also going to respectfully ask you to not step into my family's business." He spoke in a level voice, polite yet firm.

"Daniel, I'd like to point out a couple of things, my friend. First, you never bothered to ask what had happened to upset Ryan or showed any displeasure toward me on his behalf. Second, you invited me into your family business when you brought it up. And third, and most important to note, Ryan is my fated-mate. I won't hear you talk about him like that. If you have a problem with him and want to talk about it, that's fine. But I won't have him demeaned. Especially when he's not here to defend himself."

Daniel's jaw dropped as he stared at me incredulously. "Ryan? Luke's bratty little brother? The runt of the pack that walks around here doing as he pleases? He's your mate? Seriously?"

I glared at his rude descriptions of Ryan while I pushed back my bear, who had also been angered and now prowled too close to the surface. Daniel took one look at my face, and began to laugh.

He gasped out his thoughts between stretches of laughter. "Oh, shit. Ivan! I'm so sorry for you! You have no fucking idea what you're in for with that one!"

I decided that punching the Alpha's second-in-command and my future brother-in-law in the jaw wouldn't be a prudent move. My bear disagreed, but then, he wasn't the most logical of creatures. Instead, I got up and left the porch. I went next door to my room inside of the schoolhouse, with Daniel's laughter still ringing out into the night.

CHAPTER 3

RYAN

The nerve of that jerk! How dare he call me out like that? And worst of all, he'd turned me down and made me feel dirty. I mean, I didn't realize that it would piss him off like that or I might not have suggested the whole fuck-buddies thing. It had just sounded like a good idea at the time. I walked into my room, closing the door behind me, and turned the lock.

I walked unerringly through the dark, moonlit room and stripped off my clothes before I flopped down on my bed. Huh. An hour ago I was excited to spend the night with Taylor and maybe let him teach me how to fool around a little. But now the idea of letting Taylor touch me was just... wrong.

Flipping over to my side, I stared at the wall and thought about Ivan. He was so hot. And to find out that he was meant to be mine was incredible. I'd always talked a big game to Luke and anyone who would listen about how I didn't want a mate. It wasn't exactly true, though.

I wanted a mate. But I wanted a mate who would love me for myself. I didn't want someone who saw the damaged pup that had been rescued from a degrading future. I also didn't want a mate who would see me as a cute brat that knew how to get his way. And I definitely did not want to be desired because an alpha saw me as some adorable twink with a hole to plug. No. I wanted someone who would see me. Listen to me. Hold me. And most importantly, who wouldn't leave me.

My parents had died. My grandmother had died. Then I'd been through a rotating series of foster homes, yet had been lucky enough to be kept together with my brother. My final set of foster parents had sold us both to an alpha that wanted to lock us away until we were old enough to be forced into breeding pups for him. And then after all that, Luke himself had left me when he'd found Daniel.

I missed Luke more than I would ever admit out loud. Even when we'd finally had our own beds, he would always let me crawl in bed with him when the nightmares came.

He would just wrap his arms around me and hold on so tight that I almost couldn't breathe. And I'd loved it. I'd needed the grounding that it gave me to push all of the anxiety away.

But Ivan was here now. If I wanted to be brave and

accept his claim-bite, he would never leave until death took him from me. As good as that sounded, I needed to know that he wanted me as a person, not because of the pheromones that told his bear that my wolf smelled good. Or because he liked the way I looked. I wanted more.

When his arm had been around me for that brief few minutes, it was the safest that I'd ever felt in my life. But instead of telling him that, I'd been stupid. Why had I picked a fight over Taylor? I mean, I'd just met the guy!

But then I'd technically just met Ivan too. I mean, sure, I'd seen him around. But at a distance. We'd never spoken or been in the same room. But the pups all loved him, which said a lot right there. And Doc was a good guy who always spoke proudly of his son whenever Ivan came up in conversation. I knew a lot about my mate thanks to Doc's many stories.

But I'd been embarrassed when I realized that he'd seen Taylor grab my ass. And being a shifter, especially a bear with superior olfactory senses, he had smelled Taylor on me. I knew it long before Ivan mentioned it. I had been ashamed to be in the presence of my fated-mate after kissing and being touched by another. Even if he was just a friend and it didn't mean anything. It still felt like betrayal to my mate.

For the love of Fenris! What must he think of me? And then I'd followed it all up by offering to let him fuck me outside of an intended mating? Shit. It was no wonder that he'd gone all alpha on me. But instead of talking to him, I'd acted like a brat and thrown a fit, then stormed off.

If I were braver, I'd go to him now. Throw myself at him and apologize. Then beg him to take me and make me his. And never let me go. But I wasn't that brave. I pretended to be brave, but I was just needy little omega who needed a daddy after all.

Daddy, ha! I grinned suddenly, as I remembered how his eyes had flared when I'd called him that. And what was with him calling me his boy? Hmm. Next time I was about to freak out and pitch a fit because I got embarrassed around him, I was gonna ask him to spank me and see how he reacted. It wasn't like it would hurt that much, right? Who knows. I might even like it. It did sound kinda hot.

I pulled my blanket up higher, nestling in as I reached down to stroke my stiff dick and think about my tall, muscly alpha. What would it feel like to have those thick lips on mine? Would he stick his tongue in my mouth? Would those coarse whiskers he had tickle or burn? And how would it feel to have those big hands roam over my body? I bet if it was his hand stroking me right now, my dick would be swallowed in its grip.

My abs tightened and clenched, making me jerk forward as globs of hot juice shot from my slit and sprayed across my sheets into a large puddle. I sighed, and scooted back away from the proof of my release. My eyes drifted shut as I smiled and thought about what I might say when I saw Ivan tomorrow. Because yeah, I was definitely going to go knock on his door.

I woke to a loud pounding on my door. I sat up groggily and looked around. The clock beside my bed read 6:45am. Seriously? The only time I wanted to see that time was if there was a pm after it. The pounding began again. I muttered under my breath as I dragged my ass out of bed. I pulled on last night's jeans before walking over to jerk open the door. Taylor stood there with a big grin on his face.

"Wake up, precious! I'm starving and I want company when I face the pack today. Now hop to it! Hurry up and get your ass dressed." He brushed past me and came right in. After looking around, he went over and dropped down onto my bed.

I closed my eyes and sighed. Guess it was time to wake up then. Taylor talked non-stop while I got dressed. I didn't bother hiding my body from his interested eyes, but I also didn't encourage him.

As we were walking downstairs, Taylor shoulder bumped me and shot me a wink. "By the way? You should probably wash those sheets. They smell like someone was practicing his cum shots last night."

I glanced over at him and couldn't resist asking, "What's a cum shot? Or do I want to even ask?"

Taylor grinned. "Duh, virgin boy. It's what it sounds like. Shooting your wad? Blowing your load? Busting your nut? You know, when you squirt out the creamy white stuff that separates the men from the boys?"

I was giggling now. Holding up a hand, I said, "Stop! Just... ugh! No more!"

Taylor was chuckling along with me. "I could go on, but I don't wanna embarrass you in front of the pack. Or have them think that I'm as freaky as they think I look."

We reached the ground floor and I led him toward the kitchen and dining area off to the right of the stairs. "Dude. I'm pretty sure that you don't really care about either of those things."

He shrugged. "Maybe not. But I promised my brother last night that I'd try and make a good impression on everyone. So, yeah. Besides, there's bound to be pups around down here and I'm not a complete loser."

I nodded. "Yeah, not talking about my, umm, dirty laundry around the pups is probably for the best."

Taylor chortled when I said dirty laundry. We were both grinning when we entered the dining room. My smile dropped when I saw Ivan sitting at the table having coffee with Doc. I bit back a sigh and led Taylor over to the kitchen counter where Aries and Sy had spread out a buffet of breakfast foods.

They were standing there talking to each other while

dicing fruit on the other side of the counter from us. I smiled a greeting at the two older omegas, but didn't interrupt their conversation as I loaded my plate.

Now that our pack had more than doubled overnight, first-mate Kai had put new kitchen rules into place. Instead of fixing our own breakfasts and lunches now, and then coming together for a communal dinner, there would be a buffet available during certain hours. The pack omegas that lived within the lodge proper had signed up for a rotating cycle of cooking and cleaning shifts, except for the ones like me who already had jobs. The guys that lived in the cabins were exempt because they didn't eat with us.

Taylor muttered to me as he filled a plate. "This sucks, but I'm assigned clean-up duty in here when we're done eating. Apparently that's going to be my job. Well, me and my cousin. We're kitchen clean-up for all breakfast and lunch meals during the week."

I looked at him with a quirked brow. "Really? Kai assigned you guys jobs that fast? When did that happen?"

"When he showed me to my room last night. He had a clipboard with sign-up sheets for different pack duties. My cousin signed us up for clean-up when I couldn't decide on anything." He shrugged. "It's okay. Kai told me that we'd rotate on a monthly basis, so if it sucks then I'll just do something else next month."

I nodded and poured myself a cup of coffee with a shitload of cream. I took my cup and plate over to the table, noticing Ivan's eyes on me the whole time. Defiantly, I walked right over to where he sat with Doc. Taylor was right on my heels.

"Good morning, Doc!" I smiled warmly at my beloved boss. I nodded at Ivan with a polite smile, determined to make a better impression and to not to be a brat today. "Hello again, Ivan. Are you guys having a private conversation or can we join you while we eat?"

Doc answered for both of them. "Good morning, my dear Ryan. You are always welcome to join us. Please have a seat and introduce us to your friend, yes?"

"Thanks, Doc. This is Taylor, he's one of the new pack members." Turning to my friend, I motioned to the bears and said, "Taylor, this is Doc Ollie. He's our pack doctor and my boss. And you probably remember Ivan from last night."

I sat down to the right of Doc, with Taylor slipping into the seat on my other side. Ivan sat directly across from me. Shit. I hadn't thought this through. Ivan was watching me while Taylor greeted Doc. I took a bite of bacon and tried not to be nervous. Hearing Doc's proper bear cadence had made me realize all of a sudden that Ivan didn't talk like the other bears.

As if he'd read my mind, Ivan looked over at Taylor and said, "You'll notice that my father speaks more formally than the rest of us. The other bears from our den do too.

I'm a bit different from living among the humans for a decade. Although I've been known to lapse back when I spend time with just the bears."

Taylor looked over at him with interest. "Really? You lived among the humans? Why? I mean, I would love it personally. You just seem a little more traditional to me."

Doc answered for Ivan as he proudly explained. "My son went to college and then stayed to teach human children. This is fascinating, yes? We are happy that he has come back to his homelands to teach the shifter children now. It is good to have my Ivan here with me again."

Taylor spoke up, his voice muffled by a mouthful of muffin. "That's cool, Ivan." Thank Fenris, he swallowed before continuing. "Why did you come back, though? I don't know if I would've been able to do that if I was safely fitting in among the humans."

Ivan spoke patiently even though I was pretty sure that he didn't care too much for Taylor. "The humans are fine, but the big city grew too confining for my bear. I needed to come back home where I could be free to shift and let my bear roam the woods."

I nodded with complete understanding. "It's awful when you can't shift. When we first moved here, I think that my brother and I spent more time in wolf form than in our human forms."

"Why was that, Ryan?" Taylor asked curiously. I sighed, realizing that he was yet another person who didn't know my story. Doc reached over and patted my hand that rested on the table. The twinkle in his kind eyes encouraged me.

I took a fortifying drink of coffee and looked down at my plate as I spoke. "You might as well know, because you'll hear it eventually anyway. My brother and I, along with all the other original omegas here, were all rescued by Alpha Jake and his alpha friends. We'd been held captive by the old Alpha from the pack back in our old home. We were kept in a creepy little cabin in a remote area, and guarded by a nasty, mean beta wolf. He only allowed us to shift once a week."

I glanced over at Taylor's shocked face and smiled humorlessly. "And that was only if we'd been good all week. We looked forward to Sunday afternoons, but Luke and I usually screwed it up for everyone by being too loud or something. If we were good, though? We could shift as long as we stayed in the yard. We weren't allowed to run, or to wander far enough for another shifter to catch our scents."

At some point, Doc had taken my hand. He held it firmly in his, letting me draw from his alpha strength as I'd shared my story. Or, at least the parts of it that I wanted to talk about. I glanced up shyly at Ivan. He smiled gently back at me. I felt a small piece of my fractured heart mend from that sweet smile as a feeling of peace settled over me.

A hand ruffled my hair from behind, then Sy leaned over

my shoulder and said, "Tell the truth, kiddo. It was usually Luke trying to get you to stay quiet back then. But it's good that not being able to shift is the worst scar you carry from back then."

Aries spoke quietly from behind Sy. "We hated seeing you pups brought in, when Alpha Fremont dropped you off at the cabin that day. We all knew what he had planned for your future. Be glad that you were rescued while you were still young enough to come here and grow up cosseted instead of dealing with the degradation and pain that we older ones did." The two omegas came around and sat down at the table to join us with their usual cups of tea in hand.

Aries had spoken kindly enough, but his words brought home to me the fact that I really had no right to complain. I hadn't suffered nearly what he had. I mean, he had been raped more than once and forced to breed two pups that were then stolen from him. It had been a miracle when his pups were recovered after Alpha Fremont died. And poor Sy had been super pregnant and almost ready to deliver at the time of our rescue. I took a deep breath and reminded myself again that I didn't have a right to feel victimized.

But then Ivan's quiet voice spoke up. "I am horrified by what you all went through at the hands of your former Alpha. I had heard about it from my father, but I hadn't realized until now that you are all the omegas of which he spoke. Dad never told me the names of the victims, just the story of what the Alpha had done. But I wouldn't say that Ryan's worst scar is the memory of not being able to shift or to play. I am certain that is what he would have you all believe, though."

Doc spoke up and added, "Yes, it is good that this pack was able to provide a safe haven for Ryan and Luke to finish growing up. I agree with my son, though. Our Ryan is good at being playful to hide his own pain, yes? It is reasonable that you would all bear different scars. But you must remember one thing, my omega friends. You all suffered different forms of abuse, yet the pain you each carry is equally valid. I have always been grateful that these boys, who were no more than pups yet, were not forced to grow up before their time due to those awful circumstances. That would not have been a good way for a young boy to learn of adult things."

A slim pair of arms wrapped around my neck as a familiar pair of lips leaned around to peck my cheek. Kai released me after also ruffling my hair before he went over to sit down by his best friends.

"I agree with Doc. Our personal pain is all subjective to our own experiences from back then. You guys have never resented the fact that I wasn't assaulted by that Alpha ass. We all have our own pasts that pre-date our time in that cabin, and the scars from those times as well. And yeah, Ryan is probably spoiled. But can you blame any of us if we did baby him?"

"I don't know about you guys," Kai turned to look at first Sy and then Aries.

"But I always thought that Ryan and Luke were little rays of fucking sunshine in that cabin. Even when we got screwed out of yard time, it was almost worth it just to see them act like pups here and there during the week. It was ridiculous to expect two young teens like them to sit quietly and not talk."

I was stunned. Ivan, Doc, and Kai had all stood up for me. But Doc and Ivan had both also shown that they actually saw me for myself. I glanced over at Ivan. He was quietly watching me. He flashed me a private smile and a quick wink.

No one else seemed to have noticed, I thought. Until Doc gave my hand one last squeeze and pulled away. When I glanced over at Doc, his eyes were twinkling happily as they flicked back and forth from me to Ivan. So naturally, while Doc was already picking up on a vibe between me and his son, Kai had to speak up.

"So, Ryan. I never found out what you were so pissed off about last night when you came in. Rumor has it that you were bitching about some alpha. Anyone I know? I'm guessing one of the new alphas that joined the pack? Tell me, is he hot?" He leaned over the table with a big grin, waiting to hear the gossip.

Doc chuckled and took a drink of coffee while never taking his eyes off his son. I was blushing furiously, but

Ivan sat there with an impassive look on his face. His eyes were dancing with humor while he looked at me, as if waiting for my response.

I took a deep breath and turned to Kai. "It's entirely possible that I was being overly dramatic."

Kai snorted. "Is that the polite way of saying that you were pissed off and throwing a tantrum? Trust me, Squirt. I'm well versed with the proper throwing of a snit-fit. The secret is to time it effectively to achieve the desired effect." He winked. "Now, are you going to tell me who or what brought it on, or am I going to have to get Luke up here to help me tag-team tickle it out of you?"

Ivan was straight up grinning now, watching me to hear my response. "No comment, Kai. And quit pushing or I won't babysit the pups after school today."

Kai sat up then. "No! You wouldn't dare use the pups as a threat! You love my pups! Besides, Erin says that you promised to take them all out to shift in the clearing while you watch them."

He paused and looked at me with a quirked brow. "You do realize that they're all big enough to gang up on you now, right? I don't like to rough-house with those little shits without Jake nearby. The twins about ripped off my tail the last time I shifted and played with them. And Rhys? He goes right for the tail, every damn time!"

Ivan cleared his throat. "Perhaps I should join them? My

bear would love to be out in the sunshine for a change, and I could help protect the integrity of Ryan's tail."

Every eye in the room flicked over to Ivan with appraising expressions, then back to me. The interest in Kai's eyes kicked up by about thirty-seven notches.

"Hmm. That's an interesting offer, Squirt. You should consider taking Ivan up on it. The pups would love having their fabulous Mr. B out with them. The question I guess would be if you'd be equally excited for the *adult* company?" Kai smiled at me with innocent smile that didn't quite match the teasing gleam in his eyes as he purposely accented the word adult.

Ivan was either oblivious to Kai's teasing or didn't give a shit, because he chose that moment to slide his phone across the table to me. "Here, kid. Put your number in so I can text you later if I'm going to be busy after school. I never know if there's going to be a problem and I need to keep a pup afterward for detention."

Aries blushed. His daughter was a high-spirited little alpha that frequently got into trouble at school. She was a good pup. She just had problems sitting in a class all day. "I'll get Micah to join me in having a chat with Sara before school today, Ivan. She shouldn't give you any trouble, though. She's just now gotten off restriction from the last time she acted up in class."

I put my information into Ivan's phone while he chatted with Aries about Sara. I thought I was being discreet when I snapped a quick selfie to add to my contact info, but I noticed Ivan watching me out of the corner of his eye with a knowing smile. I passed his phone back with a shy grin.

Doc turned to me before anything else could happen, and clapped a hand on my shoulder. "Well, Mr. Stark, it sounds as though we ought to begin our workday. We would not want you to miss your date with my son and the Alpha's pups, yes?"

I blushed furiously at the word date, but nodded. "Sounds good, Doc. I need to get those records from last week into the computer anyway."

I turned back to Taylor, who was just finishing his breakfast. His eyes were thoughtful, as though he'd been quietly absorbing all of our interactions. "Sorry to rush off on you. Can I catch you after dinner tonight?"

He smirked at me, then glanced over at Ivan and back to me. He winked at me before answering. "Sure. Unless you get a better offer from that mystery alpha that Kai was talking about earlier. If so, just catch me later. Or I'll see you at lunch, whatever."

I heard Ivan chuckle but I ignored him as I fought a blush and said good-bye to the other omegas. Doc had already headed for the clinic.

I got up and started to clear my dishes away before following him. Taylor held a hand up. "Leave them, dude. I'll get them, I'm doing clean up in a few anyway." I smiled my thanks and turned to leave. Ivan shot me a private smile while he busily typed on his phone. I had just left the room when my phone pinged in my pocket with an incoming text.

You're definitely getting a better offer. I think we should take a run in the woods tonight. Plan on meeting me after dinner, boy.

I smiled as I sent back my response.

Bossy bear! But okay. That actually sounds good. I haven't been out for a night run in ages. Sounds like fun.

My phone pinged back almost immediately. I was reading the text as I walked into the clinic office that was conveniently located here, just right off the main living room.

So. Your last name is Stark? And mine is Black. My, my. Don't we sound like a depressing couple? We'll have to work on changing that name of yours. Soon, baby ;)

I was so intent on my phone that I walked right into Doc's back, where he was standing in front of my desk looking over our schedule. My phone went flying, but he deftly caught it mid-air. The screen was still lit up with that last text. I knew that he'd read it when he chuckled.

He handed me back the phone, tilting his head and looking at me over the top rim of his glasses. He rested a large hand gently on my shoulder and said, "I thought that I was noticing a little something between you and my son this morning. This is good, yes? I will be glad to have you join our family, Ryan. You are a good boy."

I gulped, not sure how to even respond to that one. Doc noticed, because he said, "Oh, I have embarrassed you. For this, I am sorry. This is new then? This romance with my son?" He stopped himself then and held up a hand. "Forget I said anything. I am becoming a nosy old man."

I found my voice and nervously reassured him. "No, Doc. It's okay. I'm just, umm, still getting used to the idea of Ivan. I hadn't planned on having a mate. Especially right now. But we're fated. So, I dunno. It didn't go that great when we talked last night. But maybe tonight will be better."

Doc patted my shoulder and took a step back. "This is good news, Ryan. I believe that you will be quite happy with my Ivan if you allow yourself to trust him with your heart. Give Ivan a chance, son. Do not let fear keep you from happiness, yes? This is a lesson that is unfortunately one that we all must learn with time. But take the advice of a nosy old bear. Listen more than you speak, think before you act, and allow your heart to guide you. That is all you need to know to be a good mate."

I looked up at Doc, trying to decide how to say what I was feeling. Then I just decided, *screw it,* and lunged forward. I wrapped my arms around his waist and hugged him. My cheek brushed against the soft flannel of his shirt as he gently hugged me back. I gave him a quick squeeze and stepped away, walking around to take my seat at my desk. It was past time to get to work. Enough of this feelings crap for now.

CHAPTER 4

IVAN

The day flew by, thankfully, because I was looking forward to watching Ryan play with the Alpha's pups. He hadn't responded to that last text I'd sent, not that I'd expected it. I was toying with him with that text. I wanted to see what it would take to make him accept me as his mate.

I'd wanted to cry for the boy that had been coldly sold like chattel to a perverted Alpha. When my dad reached over for his hand, it brought home to me how close they were. I knew that my dad would be happy to see me mated, but I'd wondered what he would think of my mate being so young. The amused look of appraisal he'd given me after he'd caught me winking at Ryan had answered that question for me.

And what the fuck was it with this pack? They didn't think that his captivity was enough to leave scars on his heart? Because he hadn't been raped, his experience was thought to be less valid than that of the other omegas? It was fortunate that first-mate Kai had stepped in, because I was biting back a few thoughts when the other two had spoken. They'd been kind enough, but I felt they'd belittled my mate.

And while they treated him like a pup, they teased him about being spoiled. It was no wonder that he acted like a brat. Nobody expected any more of him. Except for Dad. Dad had given him the chance to prove himself in the clinic.

And Kai. He joked and teased, but he did a good job as first-mate. He organized the household perfectly and always seemed to know what to say. I'd loved watching my boy squirm when Kai had pushed him about his fit last night.

The alarm on my phone went off, and I snapped into teacher mode. "Alright, pups. Pencils down, please." I looked over at Sara, who'd behaved so well today. She was due a reward.

"Sara, if you would be so kind as to gather everyone's tests for me?" She rose proudly to collect the tests as I continued. "Okay, little ones. You may quietly clean your desks while Sara collects your work. Once Sara has given them to me, you may gather your things and form a nice line by the door."

The young pup brought me the stack of papers. I set them on my desk and said, "Thank you, Sara. I appreciate the good example that you set for your classmates today. You may go to the front of the line, and lead your friends back to the lodge today." The job of line leader was a coveted treat. Sara's eyes lit up when I gave her the job and quickly went to get her things.

I walked over and opened the classroom door, stepping out onto the porch. I waved at Kai, who was waiting across the lawn on the porch of the lodge. He would greet the line of young ones at the other end. Except for Trixie. My friend, Karl, was waiting at the foot of our porch steps to collect his cub. They lived in a separate cabin instead of the main lodge.

I held Trixie back until the line of pups had made their way down the steps and were headed toward Kai. "Okay, Trixie. You are also dismissed, cub." She smiled up at me and then raced for Karl, throwing her chubby body into his waiting arms. I watched as Karl swung her up onto his hip, thinking of how that could be me in a few years.

"Hello, Ivan. How are you today, my friend?" Karl leaned against the stair railing and grinned up at me. "Was Miss Trixie a good pupil today?"

"Miss Trixie is always good, Karl. Aren't you, cub?" Trixie nodded her head so fast that her curls were bouncing.

Karl kissed her cheek and then looked up at me with a knowing smirk. "So, Ivan. My mates and I noticed a certain young omega was mighty perturbed last night. I do not know how much of his mutterings that the wolves heard, but I was able to hear every word as he stomped upstairs."

I gave him a wry grin. "Really, Karl? Are you asking me a question or gossiping? I surely don't know what he could have been muttering about when I was outside, now could I?"

Karl shook his head. "You are not going to tell your oldest friend that you have found the one for you? I am offended, Ivan."

I rolled my eyes. "No, you're not. You're just nosy is what you are. But as you know yourself, finding your mate and convincing them to accept you are two different things altogether."

Karl nodded sagely. "Just be glad that you only have the one to convince, yes?"

I chuckled, leaning back against the wall of the building as I shoved my hands in my pockets. I glanced at the cub, but she had dozed off against Karl's shoulder. "Daniel pissed me off after that. He showed no concern for what had upset the young man, but instead wanted to tell me that he's a spoiled brat. When I cautioned him that he was speaking about my mate, he just fucking laughed."

Karl smirked. "And then you punched him, yes?"

"Please. I have more control over my bear than that. But

yeah, I definitely thought about it. I went home instead. He was still laughing when I left."

Karl shook his head. "It is difficult for your mate. The pack has known him since he was a pup. It has occurred to me on occasion that Ryan behaves the way that they expect him to, but I have kept it to myself. His brother and Daniel are my neighbors, as you know. We were over there a lot after Luke had the triplets. They both treat him as a child, yet rely on him to help care for the babes. I do not think they mean to take advantage, yet they do. It will be good for him to have an alpha at his side now, yes?"

I nodded grimly. "Yeah. It's tough. But I know his brother loves him, and is used to being the one to watch over him. I told Daniel that I don't think that he and his mate know Ryan as well as they think they do."

Karl grinned. "I imagine that was well received, yes?"

I chuckled. "Yeah, about as well as a fart at the dinner table. But screw it, I'm going to protect him and stand up for him. I wouldn't be much of an mate or an alpha if I didn't, you know?"

Karl nodded. "Well, I wish you the best of luck. Enjoy the chase, my friend. I have a feeling that your young man will lead you around in circles before he submits to a claim. That one is a stubborn wolf. He's had to be, given his childhood."

"And why am I the only one that didn't know about my

mate's childhood? I wasn't happy with the things I learned this morning, about how he came to join this pack."

Shaking his head sadly, Karl replied, "That was a terrible situation. My Owen has told me about the night when they found them all. He was one of the team that rescued those omegas. He said that the young Stark boys' presence there was bone chilling. It was good that they were able to come here, and finish growing up peacefully. And, Ivan? Perhaps the reason that you do not know more about your mate is because you keep yourself shut away in your schoolhouse much of the time."

I nodded with chagrin. "Yeah, well, that will be changing. In fact, I should get going because I have plans to help Ryan babysit for the Alpha."

Karl grinned broadly. "Ah. That is a perfect date. He will be at ease with the pups. And not able to argue in front of them. You are a smart man, my friend."

I shrugged. "I just saw an opportunity to spend time with him and took it. The real date is planned for after dinner when we go for a moonlit run."

"Ah, yes. That is a much better date. So, you are suggesting that my mates and I go for a run tonight, yes?" He chuckled as my eyes narrowed.

"Karl, I love you like a brother. But if your furry ass shows up in those woods tonight, I will take you down!"

Karl laughed and waved a hand at me as he turned to head home. He called back over his shoulder, "Good luck, my friend. I will be rooting for you!"

I snorted and turned to go back inside to put the papers away to grade later. I was smiling as I went around the classroom, pushing in chairs and cleaning up from the day. I knew that Karl would be back tomorrow looking for a full accounting of my date. Nosy damned shifter.

———

Ryan's wolf was as sleek and fit as his human counterpart. I had already shifted as I lumbered across the parking lot to where Ryan played with the Alpha's four pups in the afternoon sun. The sunlight shone against his glossy fur as he ran around in the grass.

His chocolate brown coat was a reflection of the dark brown, nearly black hair he had in human form. On his wolf though, the colors were a rich symphony of various shades of brown with a hint of red top notes and black undertones that peeked through as the breeze ruffled his coat. His fur looked like it would be thick and silky to the touch. I imagined that it would be perfect to run my fingers through, if I were in my human form.

The four of them were chasing Ryan around in a circle as I approached. I noticed how careful he was with them, especially the little pudgy one. Erin and the twins were all students of mine, but the littlest pup was too young for school just yet. He was obviously an alpha. His older siblings were wild and playful, but he stalked after Ryan as if hunting prey.

It was adorable to watch. I wasn't sure how old he was exactly. Two? Maybe three? Somewhere in there. It would be amusing to see how he changed as he grew. The little guy pounced right then, launching himself at Ryan's tail. I chuffed out my bear's version of a laugh, remembering Kai's warning this morning.

While Ryan tried to dislodge the scamp, the other three tackled him, taking him down into a dog-pile. I watched him try to break free from the wriggling pups until he gave up and flopped limply beneath them.

I walked over then, picking the pups off him one by one, carrying them gently by the scruff of their necks as I sat them down to the side. I gave them a stern glance, but it was unnecessary. Simply the presence of an alpha bear was enough to still them for now. I removed the little alpha last, amused as he instinctively kicked at my jaw and fought for release. His omega siblings had all gone limp in my hold, but not this little one. He was going to fight me every inch.

When I put him down, rather than sit calmly and cower, he immediately jumped at me. Yipping at me adorably, he jumped up on his back paws and tried to swipe at me with his front ones. I batted back at him playfully, my claws safely retracted. Before long, his siblings were joining in.

Ryan regained his energy and tag-teamed with the pups in their efforts to take me down. I don't know how long we played until the Alpha's car pulled up and parked in front of the lodge. Alpha Jake and Kai got out and came walking over, hand in hand.

I was flopped on my side at that point, with Erin and the twins laying over my back. The little alpha pup was half-heartedly gnawing on Ryan's tail where he lay panting a few feet away from me.

Alpha Jake snapped his fingers with a wide grin. All four pups jerked to attention and ran over to greet their parents. Kai shook his head and simply said, "Shift, please."

They all shifted in a blur of color, fur, and skin before they finally stood there as human children. They immediately began talking over each other as they happily greeted their dads, telling them about their afternoon.

Ryan rolled over and smoothly transitioned to his human form. I stayed as a bear. Not only did I prefer to stay where I was, enjoying the heat of the sun baking my fur, but I didn't think it prudent for my students to see their teacher naked. As shifters, nudity is accepted as common and natural. Really, there's not much to be done when we all lose our clothing in the shift and come back nude.

Perhaps it was due to the decade I'd spent among the humans, but I preferred to keep that part of myself private. After they left, I would go back around behind the schoolhouse and shift near my private entrance. No lodge windows overlooked the area where I preferred to shift, and the door to my room was well hidden from view. This was thanks to the trees the stood behind the schoolhouse cabin that contained the classroom and my private living quarters.

I tuned out the conversation of the Alpha family, choosing instead to let my eyes roam over Ryan's lithe form. It was horrible etiquette for a shifter to ogle another one post-shift before they dressed. I thought that rule might not apply in this situation, though. After all, Ryan would be my mate. It was just a matter of when.

Just when I thought that I would never see anything hotter than his tightly rounded buttocks and smooth back, he turned. With one hand on his hip, he glared down at me knowingly. Gads, he might be a petite man, but he packed a lot of muscle on that slim form. I couldn't wait to run my tongue over the peaks and valleys of his toned stomach.

Just as I started to eyeball his perky prick and taut little sac, he waved a hand in front of my face. Pointing to his own face, Ryan taunted me. "Eyes up here, perv. Sheesh. Do you have no manners? Next thing I know, you'll be trying to rub all up on me or something."

Rising to my feet, I took him up on his suggestion as I lazily rubbed up against him, marking him firmly with my scent. He listed slightly to the side, but dug his heels into the grass to hold himself upright against my large size. Ryan glared at me, and my pointy bear snout snuffled into his neck as I ran my tongue over his omega gland.

"Ugh! Boundaries, much? Stinky bear breath," he muttered, trying to cover the scent of arousal that was already wafting from him. I chuffed and walked past him. I noticed Alpha Jake watching me stake my claim with barely-hidden glee, while Kai's jaw was dropped down somewhere in the vicinity of his knees.

I headed home, leaving Ryan to field the flurry of questions that Kai was sure to ask. It was unfortunate, but since I didn't want to flash my naked body to the pups, there was no choice but to leave.

Once I'd shifted, I quickly slipped into my living quarters. I pulled on a pair of cargo shorts and snagged my phone to shoot off a text.

I do not have bear breath. Or maybe I do? Don't forget our date tonight. I'll be by the lodge at 8 to pick you up. Looking forward to some alone time. ;)

I shoved my phone into my pocket and padded into the adjoining schoolroom to grade the tests and papers from today's lessons. After I'd finished that, I would make a sandwich or something for dinner before I went to round up my omega for a moonlit stroll through the woods.

I smiled to myself. It looked as though things were headed in the right direction for our mating. If things went well tonight, I could be mated as soon as the weekend. Well, as long as nothing went wrong and Ryan was agreeable.

CHAPTER 5

RYAN

The rest of the evening was a nightmare. Naturally Kai had a lot of questions about me and Ivan. When I'd grudgingly admitted that he was my fated-mate, Alpha Jake had tossed me over his shoulder and spun me in a circle, crowing loudly.

Of course, this went down in the main living room of the lodge. And naturally most of our friends were there to witness it. I mean, why couldn't I have a little bit of privacy to sort this shit out and make up my mind about Ivan? I said as much to Kai, but he'd just laughed at me.

"Make up your mind? Yeah, you do that, squirt. But let me clue you in on a little secret. Putting off your mate now that you found him will only piss off your wolf. And you'll never find anyone else that will make you feel the same way. In fact, you'll feel dirty even thinking of seeing someone else, now that you've found your fated-mate."

I rolled my eyes. "Are you being for real right now? Or is this just something that they tell us little omegas so that we bow down gracefully and accept the alpha's bite?"

"Oh, man. You're cynical for such a young guy," Seth said from where he sat on the couch with Sy curled up on his lap. "Ryan, ask anyone here. We alphas are just as screwed as you omegas once we meet our fated-mates. I couldn't look at anyone else once I'd caught Sy's scent." He glanced apologetically at Sy before saying, "Why do you think that those two years when Sy wouldn't accept me were so miserable? Trust me on this one, Ryan. You'll be hurting Ivan as much as yourself if you push him away."

Sy added, "And that might sound like it sucks right now, like you're stuck getting mated to some random alpha just because you caught each other's scent. But take it from me? Not accepting him will make your wolf crazy, and make you lonelier than you ever thought possible. Your spirit has found its other half, so you'll feel the push to join."

I rolled my eyes. "Yeah, but after we join and have sex, then what? Then I'm stuck forever without ever having really lived."

Kai put his arm around my shoulders and pulled me against his slim frame. "Ryan, you won't really live until you have your mate. It's hard to understand, but having that one person who completely understands you and has your back no matter what? That's really living. Everything before Jake was a half-life. Once we claimed each other, it was as if color bled into my life after a lifetime of living in black and white."

Jake spoke from over Kai's shoulder. "Kai's right, kiddo. You need to trust Ivan. He won't be able to hurt you any more than you would want to hurt him. You'll understand that once you've bonded. True-mates feel each other's pain, and can feel their emotions. It may sound scary that you won't be able to hide from him, but by the same token, he won't be able to hide from you either. Mating is about being vulnerable to each other, and also being secure in each other."

Of course, that's when I realized that my brother and his family had slipped in while I'd been listening to Jake. Daniel looked apologetic, as he stood there with a baby in each arm. Luke stormed over to me, while our friends watched in shocked silence. Nobody spoke, but just stood there and watched our brotherly drama unfold.

After handing the baby on his hip to Kai, Luke turned and glared at me silently. We stood there glaring at each other for a long awkward moment, then he finally raised a finger and pointed toward the stairs. I shook my head, prepared to stand my ground. But as I opened my mouth to speak, Luke clenched his jaw and ground out between his gritted teeth, "Upstairs, Ryan. We are speaking privately. Go."

Feeling once again like the loser kid brother, I ducked my head down and went up the stairs to my room. When we got there, I flopped down on my bed. I sat there, elbows on knees and head in hands, while Luke paced back and forth bitching at me.

"Why, Ryan? Why did I have to hear from my mate that you've apparently found yours? And he had to hear it from your intended, not from your lips. Do you have no concept of family? Are you that fucking selfish? What the hell, Ryan? It's not that I don't want you to have a mate, although I do think that you have a hell of a lot of growing up to do before you even consider a claim. And now you've told the whole damned pack before coming to me and asking what I think about this relationship?"

Once he started winding down, I looked up and asked dryly, "Are you finished, or did you have more bullshit to fling before I get to speak?"

"No! You do not get to pull your spoiled shit with me, Ryan Nathan Stark! I've known you for your entire life! What makes you think that you're ready to mate? And especially with an older, serious bear like Ivan?" Luke was vibrating with outrage.

"No, Luke. You can stop right there." I stood up and got right in my brother's face. "There's the same age difference with us as there is between you and Daniel. And did I give you any shit about that? No. I was happy for you. And for someone with a fated-mate, you sure are acting like I had a choice in who and when Fenris decided to drop mine in my lap!"

"Wait. Hold on. Daniel didn't say that you were fated. That's different." Luke had the grace to blush with shame. "I still think that you're too young and immature, though."

"Luke, sit your hypocritical ass down and listen." I hid my shock as my brother took a seat at the edge of my bed and actually seemed willing to hear me out. "First, I never even said whether I was planning on accepting or denying him. I literally just scented him last night, and that didn't end well." Luke grinned, obviously having heard Daniel's retelling of the events of the night before.

"And I'd just like to point out that I'm not much younger than you were when you accepted Daniel." I held up a hand as he opened his mouth to speak. "I know that I'm just your loser kid brother that you think is too spoiled and immature to mate, but maybe you should stop for a second and think about it. Fenris is the one that decides when we meet our fated-mates. Surely the god that you believe in must know more about me than you do, hmm? He obviously thinks that I can handle this, if he chose to give me Ivan right now." I sighed and went to sit down beside him.

"I didn't call you or come by today because I was working. And then I'd promised to watch the pups while Kai and Alpha Jake went to town for a while. I was going to come over tomorrow."

He eyed me slowly, then nodded. "Why not tonight?"

I grinned. "Because tonight I have a date to go for a moonlight walk in the forest with Ivan. Sorry, Luke. But that offer sounded way better than coming over and watching you and Daniel change diapers all evening."

"Ryan? I don't think you're a loser. I'm sorry if I've ever made you feel that way. I just..." He stopped with a sigh and hung his head for a moment before continuing. "Ryan, I've spent your whole life looking after you. It's really hard to stop now. And then I was getting texts from everyone earlier, teasing me about my new brother-in-law? Yet you, my own brother, hadn't even said a word. I don't like how we're growing apart, runt. I hate it. And then I came in just now and heard everyone advising you to jump into this claim that will take you away from me forever? I just kinda lost my shit. I'm sorry."

I reached over and took his hand. "Luke? We're not growing apart, we just grew up. And Ivan isn't taking me away from you, any more than Daniel took you from me. It is what it is, you know? Part of growing up and making life changes. You think that I didn't feel any of this when you got mated and then had the Trips?"

I squeezed my brother's hand and caught his eye. "And Luke? Please understand me when I tell you this, okay? I don't need you to be responsible for me, or try to parent me. You have the Trips for that shit. I'm your brother, not your oldest pup."

Luke giggled. "Could have fooled me with the way that you act sometimes!"

With a sigh, I nodded regretfully. "Yeah, and I need to own that. It's easier to act like a little shit sometimes than it is to actually open up to people. Even you. But I don't want to be that guy anymore. I also want you to know that I appreciate how you've always looked after me, and been there for me. But now? Now I need for you to be my friend, and my big brother that I can talk to about shit, okay?"

Luke nodded and reached over to hug me. His chin rested on my shoulder as he held me in a firm embrace and began to speak. "You know, what the guys were saying downstairs is true. I think you should go for it, Ryan. Ivan is a good man, and you were right when you said that Fenris wouldn't have put you guys in each other's path if you weren't ready for the next step in your life."

I sighed softly against his ear. "I know. It's just scary. And all this talking shit is just multiplied times a thousand with him! And even when he isn't talking, like today when he was in bear form while I babysat? His eyes still expressed volumes. I've never had anyone totally interested in me like this before, it's kinda weird."

Luke released me and sat back with a dry chuckle. "Yeah, it's really intense when you meet your fated-mate. And not to freak you out, but when you claim each other, you'll be able to somewhat read each other's minds and know what each other is feeling. It gives a whole new meaning to open communication, let me tell you!"

I bit my lip and looked off vacantly as I mulled that over. It didn't freak me out like he'd probably thought it would. The idea that Ivan would honestly be able to completely know me and read my feelings made me feel warm all over. All I'd ever wanted was for someone to truly know me. This mating thing sounded better and better.

I gave my brother another hug and stood up. "Are we good now? Can we go have dinner? Because like I said, I have a date tonight. But I'd like it if you guys stayed and had dinner with the pack. I miss seeing you at the table. "

"Yeah, how's that gonna work now that the pack has doubled?" Luke asked as he stood up and started sniffing the air.

"Oh, Kai organized it so that meal times are assigned now. We all drew from a hat last night for our official meal times. Except breakfast. That's an open buffet. And he left space in the different seatings in case we have visitors or some of you come up from your cabins." I was heading for the door, and opened it as I spoke.

"Wow, Kai is really good at that shit, isn't he?" Luke stopped and bent back over my bed. I froze, my face turning bright red as I realized what he'd been sniffing. He turned back to me with a grossed-out look on his face and said, "Really, Ryan? You jerked off in your bed and then let me sit on your dried splooge? That's just nasty."

I'd honestly forgotten all about it. My blush turned into nervous giggles that quickly morphed into hardcore, side splitting laughs as Luke glared and pushed past me indignantly. I followed him downstairs, laughing the whole way.

———

After a surprisingly nice dinner with my brother and our core group of friends, I said good-night and headed upstairs with the intention of showering and changing for my date. I didn't know if we were walking in human form or running in animal form, so I figured I'd be ready either way. That was when the rest of my night went to hell.

I'd just made it the second floor landing when Taylor came down from the top floor with another omega. I stopped to say hello, and to greet the new omega. He was a little taller than Taylor, about my own height. He had neatly combed blond hair and thick glasses. I tried not to smirk at his sweater vest and corduroy pants.

It made sense when Taylor introduced him. "Hey, Ry! Meet Walter, my cousin and roommate. We have kitchen duty in an hour, but Walt wanted to go downstairs and meet more of the pack."

I smiled and held out a hand to the nerdy looking omega. "Hey, Walter. It's nice to meet you. Are you liking it here so far?"

Walter sniffed, as though he had allergies, and shook my hand. "Hello, Ryan. It's nice to finally put a face to your name. My cousin has been filling my ear about his new friend." He smiled shyly and released my hand. Digging into his pocket, he pulled out a handkerchief and abruptly blew his nose. Loudly.

I bit the inside of my cheek to keep from giggling at the look of disgust on Taylor's face. Taylor rolled his eyes and said, "Pardon Walt. He has bad allergies."

"Really? I didn't know that was a thing with shifters," I said curiously.

Walter shoved the wadded hankie back into his pocket and explained in a nasal voice. "I'm actually a halfling. My father was human. I'm able to achieve a shift, but I'm unfortunately plagued with human illnesses and seasonal allergies. I probably need to adapt to the pines around here or invest in some allergy medicine."

My eyes bugged out. "Really? That's so cool! I've never met a halfling. I mean, I am sorry to hear about your allergies. But super cool on being a halfling, Walter!"

"My goodness! Isn't that interesting? I'll have to interview you, son. It will be good information for my books." I turned to see the Alpha's Aunt Kat walking up the stairs behind us. She was a hilarious old lady that actually made a lot of money writing sexy shifter romance books. Aunt Kat also had a successful blog and website that discussed and sold sexual aids and adult toys.

"Hi, Aunt Kat." I greeted her with a side hug. With my arm around her shoulders, I introduced her to Taylor and Walt.

She eye-balled Taylor and said, "You are intriguing, young man. Have you ever tried nipple clamps?"

Taylor choked at that, his face turning bright red. Yeah, Aunt Kat was an acquired taste. Poor Walter looked like he was about to faint. I quickly explained about Aunt Kat's books and website, while trying not to laugh. When he'd regained his composure, Walter excused himself and eased around us before dashing downstairs.

"Aunt Kat! You scandalized that poor man!" I scolded her teasingly with a grin on my face. "But tell me, what makes you ask about something like that anyway? What exactly are nipple clamps and why would anyone want to use them? Did you have Kai try them yet?"

She started excitedly telling me about how she'd ordered some for a scene in her new book. Aunt Kat loved to test out the items she used in her books. Usually Kai was her guinea pig, though.

"Oh, sweetie! Have you got a lot to learn! Some people like a little pain with their pleasure, honey. You never know, you might enjoy some nipple stimulation. You'll never know if you don't try! But it'd be easier to show you than to tell you. You boys come to my office and I'll get them out."

She took a few steps, then looked back to see us still standing there. "Well, come on! It's just a sex aid, boys. Nothing to be afraid of, trust me. Although, I'm ashamed to admit that my sweet Kai refused to do this particular little experiment for me."

We followed her to her office. Taylor looked intrigued now, but I was definitely reluctant. I mean, what would Ivan think? But Aunt Kat was a force of nature. Before I knew it, she had our shirts off and we were kneeling in front of her desk with our nipples being pinched by little metal devices. Taylor wore a small pair that she called clothespin clamps, while mine were longer ones that she'd referred to as tweezer clamps.

"Now I have those at the loosest setting on each of you, but I can tighten the screw and increase the pressure on yours, Taylor. Ryan, yours are easily adjusted by sliding that little ring around the arms. You push it down for more intensity, from what I've been told. Now please, tell me your impressions," she said with an expectant smile. Aunt Kat turned and picked up a note pad and pen, ready to take notes.

Taylor spoke up first. "I like it, ma'am." He blushed lightly as he spoke to the sweet looking little woman. "It's like this intense, pinching type of feeling that sends a shot of electricity straight to my cock."

Aunt Kat nodded happily as she recorded his thoughts. "And would you like them tighter, do you think?" I looked over at his pink nipples, thinking how painful those clamps looked. Mine weren't that bad though, so who knows? "And Ryan? What do you think, dear?"

I was about to answer when I saw movement at the corner of my eyes. Looking up, I nearly threw up when I saw Ivan's thunderous expression as he took in the scene. Alpha Jake and Kai were there with him. Ivan abruptly turned and stalked away. Alpha Jake looked at his aunt and asked dryly, "Another experiment, Auntie?"

"Why, yes, dear boy! I cornered these young men and got them to help me out. Why? Did you and Kai decide to help me after all? I have more sets that we can use!"

The Alpha rolled his eyes. He turned to Kai. "Rescue them, I'm gonna go explain about my aunt to Ivan before he goes off and tears something apart."

Aunt Kat looked worried as she asked Kai, "Is there a problem? Should I not have asked them?"

Kai sighed and pinched the bridge of his nose. "Guys, please just take those ridiculous things off and get your shirts on. Taylor, go get dinner before your shift in the kitchen. Ryan, go find your man, but maybe wait a few minutes. Let Jake calm him down first."

Taylor carefully removed his clamps and went to hand them to Aunt Kat. She held up a palm and shook her head. "Wait, you said that you enjoyed them? Keep them with my thanks. Maybe we can chat more tomorrow?" She winked at him and added, "The information I read said that they're also a fantastic masturbatory aid."

Taylor pocketed them with a grin and pulled his shirt down over his slightly swollen nipples. He leaned forward and pecked her cheek. "Thanks, ma'am. I'd be happy to talk to you more tomorrow. We can experiment with tightening them if you want." He winked and swaggered out the door.

Kai shook his head and turned to Aunt Kat. "That alpha that was with us is Ryan's fated mate. He was looking around for his father before he met Ryan for a date they have planned tonight." Kai glanced over at me, where I still knelt with the clamps on. I'd been too shocked to move during this whole ordeal. "Aunt Kat, can you please remove those ridiculous things from the kid?"

Kai stepped over to her desk chair and dropped down into it. "Ryan, you're so lucky that Alpha and I were with Ivan. Until you guys are claimed, his bear is going to be too close to the surface where you're concerned. You can't tease him like that."

Aunt Kat removed the clamps and I pulled my shirt on over my numb nipples. "I didn't, I mean, that is..." I was at a loss for words and ready to cry from frustration.

Kai smiled gently at me. "It's okay, Ryan. Go find your alpha, explain that Jake's crazy aunt shanghaied you, and work it out. The best way to fix a problem with your mate is through good communication. Remember that."

Aunt Kat nodded. "Exactly right, Kai. And Ryan? I'm so sorry, dear. I had no idea that you had a mate that was ready to claim you. I never would have asked you to do this right now if I had."

"It's okay, Aunt Kat. I could have said no. I guess I didn't think it would bug him that much." I smiled and took a deep breath before heading for the door.

"Oh, Ryan?" I looked back at Aunt Kat. "You didn't say. I need to know if you had the same response that Taylor did or did you want yours tighter?"

Kai gasped, but I just grinned cheekily at the little lady. "They were fine, but mostly just made me feel numb. If that helps?"

"Oh, yes! Thank you! Let me know if you want to try them again, or even another product! I have lots of fun things, especially if you're about to get mated." She scribbled notes on her tablet, while talking distractedly. I slipped out of the room while I could and left Kai alone with her.

CHAPTER 6

IVAN

The worst part about what I'd just seen was that I was equal parts turned on and pissed as hell. Oh, I knew all about Aunt Kat from my dad. I also knew that she'd likely dragged both of the omegas in there to test out her latest toys. I was just pissed because the peacock had been there too, and he'd had a strong scent of arousal coming off him.

I hadn't scented the same from Ryan, which was the only reason that I didn't go ape shit on the spot. Instead, I'd removed myself from the situation. I walked out onto the front porch and dropped down onto my favorite bench. Moments later, the screen door creaked open and Alpha Jake stepped out.

He walked over. "Is it okay to sit, or are you ready to kill someone right now."

I grunted out a laugh and scrubbed a hand over my face.

"Naw, man. It's cool. I'm not going to kill anyone or break anything."

Alpha raised a brow and smirked. "Are you sure? Because if that had been Kai before I'd claimed him? I probably wouldn't have reacted so calmly." He sighed. "I take it that you know about my aunt and her eccentricities?"

I chuckled. "Yeah, Dad's told me a few stories over the years. Your aunt sounds like a peach or something."

Alpha shook his head. "Oh, Aunt Kat is something all right. But she means well. She just doesn't always think about how other people might react to her experiments."

"Don't worry about it, Alpha," I said calmly.

"Jake. When we're alone, I'd like to think that we're friends enough now that you can call me by name, Ivan." Jake smiled wryly as I nodded.

"Okay, then don't worry about it, *Jake*," I said with a snort of laughter. "Honestly. I knew what was happening the minute I saw him in there. And I'm sure that he wasn't a volunteer so much as tricked into it. No offense," I said with a grin.

"Oh, don't worry. None taken. Besides, she admitted that she'd cornered them as soon as I asked." He shrugged. "She's quirky, but like I said, she means well."

I flapped a hand at him. "Don't worry. I was just pissed off because that shitty little peacock smelled turned on as hell and I didn't like it."

Jake snorted and threw his head back with a shout of laughter. "Shitty little peacock? Oh, fuck! That's awesome!" He laughed some more, wiping his eyes before he continued. "Although, as Alpha, I really shouldn't be laughing at that hysterically accurate depiction of a pack member."

I shrugged. "Hey, funny is funny. But yeah. That little shit grabbed my boy's butt right in front of me while they both smelled like they'd been fooling around." I didn't like to talk about my mate, but I needed to tell someone and I knew it wouldn't go any further than Jake. Besides, he probably should know this about the new omega.

"Yeah, I've heard a few rumors about him. Apparently, he's restless and more than a little wild. He seems like a good kid though, just needs a little direction. My mate is planning to keep a close eye on him, with the help of his cousin that Daniel and Kai conveniently made him room with when we assigned rooms. I'm sure they were just experimenting. Ryan's a good kid, with a big heart. I imagine that he was probably not the aggressor. In fact, I'd lay odds on that one."

I nodded. "Yeah. And I know the peacock's another omega and not worth getting jealous over, but my bear is restless so I'm less patient than I otherwise would be." I stood and stretched. "Jake, I appreciate you following me down to talk. I was supposed to go on a date in the woods with Ryan tonight, but I imagine that he's probably too embarrassed to come down here now. If you see him, tell him I went home, okay?"

Jake nodded and stood to shake my hand. "Alright, Ivan. Hang in there, man. I'm sure that you and Ryan will figure things out soon enough."

I nodded and made my exit, quickly moving across the grass and letting myself into the schoolhouse. So much for date night, I thought with a sigh.

Minutes later, there was a light knock on my private entrance. I knew it was Ryan, I could smell him through the wall. Damn. If his scent was that potent, it meant that his first heat was drawing near. I didn't want to mate him for the very first time during heat. I wanted it to be special.

Opening the door, I looked down at a sheepish looking Ryan. "Can we talk?" he asked as he pushed past me and let himself into my room. I closed the door and turned to look at him as he paced back and forth. I leaned against the door, shoving my hands into my pockets while I waited for the tantrum to commence.

Surprisingly though, he calmly walked over and stopped in front of me. "Are you mad at me? Is this where you go all Daddy alpha bear and throw me over your knees for a good spanking? Because we can go there if it will help you forgive me. I'm sorry. I didn't mean to offend you or upset your bear."

He raised his anxious eyes at me. I looked into those

chocolate colored orbs and smiled gently. "I'm not mad. There's nothing to forgive, Ryan. I know all about Aunt Kat and her crazy antics. I wasn't thrilled to see the peacock there and all turned on like he was, but that's not on you."

Ryan blushed. "He wasn't turned on by me, if it helps. It was those clampy things. Taylor said it sent a shot of electricity straight to his cock and..." I held a hand up and covered his mouth.

"Please, I don't want to ever the hear the words Taylor and cock in a sentence again." I shuddered, trying to block the ick factor from my brain. Ryan helped distract me when I felt his tongue lick my palm.

I pulled my hand away quickly. "What the fuck? Did you just lick me, omega boy?"

Ryan's eyes flashed fire. "Yes. I did. I do not like to be silenced, and I never like to have my mouth covered or my hands bound. Sorry, that's just a hard no thanks to my childhood. Now, can we agree to stop with the boy shit? Or are we back to the whole Daddy thing?" He tilted a hip and crossed his arms over his chest as he glared up at me.

Looking down at him, I hung my head with chagrin. "Oh, hell. I'm sorry. I never even thought about you possibly having a problem with my hand over your mouth that. I just wanted you to stop talking. And I don't honestly mean the whole boy thing in a derogatory way. I mean, you're my omega, and you're my guy, right? But it's weird to call you guy. It's no different than when men call women they're dating their 'girl'. I just meant it in a special way, like an affectionate nickname, you know? But if it bothers you, I'll drop it. Forgive me?"

Ryan dropped his arms and stepped forward to wrap his arms around my waist. My arms immediately went around him as he looked up at me with his chin resting between my pecs.

"I forgive you, Ivan. And I don't care if you call me your boy, as long as you don't think of me as a kid. I'm trying to show you here that I can actually adult like a real grown-up." He grinned up at me cheekily. "I even had an actual conversation with my brother earlier. I'll tell you about it later. Right now, I have a few things to say to you first."

"Should I be afraid?" I asked with a smile as I reached a hand up to push a loose lock of hair behind his ear. Just as I'd imagined when he was in wolf form, his human hair was soft and silky to the touch.

"No, Ivan. I did a lot of thinking last night. You were right. If I want to be treated like an adult, I need to act like one. Maybe if I'd shown a little more discretion and acted a lot less like a spoiled brat last night, the whole pack wouldn't have known about our private business before we were ready to announce it." His eyes glowed in the soft light of my room. I could spend all night just staring into those luminous pools.

"Ryan, it's okay. We have nothing to hide. We're shifters, babe. It's normal to mate. And I'm glad that you took the time to think about all this and come to this realization on your own. That's more mature than a lot of adults I've known, so you don't need to worry. You're *adulting* just fine."

"I came to a few other realizations too." He looked up at me with a furrowed brow as his lip automatically formed into that now familiar pout. "I realized that I need you. Not because I need an alpha's knot," he blushed, "but because I'm sick of being alone. And of everyone I love either dying or leaving. I've never in my life had anyone who saw me for myself, or at least that's what I thought."

He pulled back and grabbed my hand, guiding me to the foot of the bed and taking a seat. I sat down beside him quietly, allowing him to finish. "I realized today that Doc sees me. And on some levels, Kai sees me. But you? You see me completely. You called me on my shit last night, and didn't back down. I was totally shitty last night! Yet you still wanted to be with me today, even when I was playing with the pups. I feel safe with you, even though you're a friggin' huge alpha bear. You make me feel free to be myself without having to play a role. If that's what being a mate is, then I'm all in."

"That is exactly what being a mate is, Ryan. It means always having your back, but allowing you the freedom to be yourself. And you weren't completely shitty last night,

I was egging you on. I thought your tantrum was adorable."

I stopped and grinned down at him before I continued. "But I know that's not who you are. You're a hard working young man that's had a lot more shit happen in his life than anyone deserves. You have a lot more to offer than many people give you credit for, but that's going to change. I won't have people making any kind of derogatory comments about you." I stopped, gathering my thoughts. "I'm glad that you came here ready to have a real conversation. Did you really mean it when you said that you were in about us mating?"

Ryan nodded. "I did. I don't want to be without you, now that I've found you. Like I told my brother. If Fenris decided it was time for us to meet and discover that we were mates, then he knew that I was ready. If it's good enough for a god, it's good enough for me. So yeah, I'm ready and willing to be yours if you'll have me."

I chuckled at his raw honesty. "We'll circle back to you telling Luke all that at another time. Right now? I definitely want to have you and keep you for my mate."

I patted my leg. "Come here, Ryan. Sit on my lap, my bear needs me to touch you while we talk, if that makes sense."

Ryan smiled at my words and stood up, kicking off his shoes. To my complete shock, he then shucked his shirt and flung it over his shoulder without ever losing eye contact with me. I about swallowed my tongue as he slowly stripped off his pants. It wasn't a professional strip show, but it didn't need to be. This was my mate, baring himself for my eyes only.

Ryan walked over and swung a leg over my lap as he grabbed my shoulders and settled himself into place so that he was facing me. I reverently ran the back of my hand over his cheek, stroking his soft skin.

His luminous chocolate orbs filled with wonder as he looked up at me. Framing his face with my hands, I leaned forward and gently pressed my lips to his. Ryan tilted his head and accepted my kiss, kissing me back passionately. His mouth opened, and I slipped my tongue into it touch his.

Arms came up to wrap around my neck as I slid my hands down his back and cupped his ass, holding him against me while we kissed. Ryan was kissing me so passionately, it was as if he were trying to steal the very oxygen from my lungs. I broke the kiss, leaning back to gasp for breath.

"Damn, baby. Do I want to know how you learned to kiss like that?" I asked him with a smirk. My hands still cupped his ass, my thumbs stroking small circles over the dimples that dipped in just above his ass cheeks.

He blushed, and looked down as if ashamed while shaking his head no. "I doubt it, so maybe we can just forget it? I mean, it was only one stupid kiss that didn't mean anything. But I'm sorry it wasn't with you."

Fucking peacock. I knew that without asking. Instead, I reached a hand around and tipped his chin up with two fingers. "I don't care that I wasn't the first man you've kissed, baby. As long as I'm the last. Besides, it would be hypocritical of me if I minded. It's not like I never kissed anyone else myself."

Ryan's eyes narrowed, but his shoulders relaxed and he nodded. "You're right. Let's forget about past experiences and just focus on being together. I'm not going to be a brat about things that I can't change."

"I thought you were hanging up the brat hat now anyway?" I smirked with a raised brow.

"But if I'm never a brat," he said as looked up at me flirtatiously from under his lashes, "how will I ever get to role-play with you and let Daddy give me a spanking?"

My jaw dropped. "You weren't joking about that?" My mind raced into filthy directions as I pictured how pretty those cheeks would look flushed red with my hand prints on them.

He wiggled his butt with a coy smile. "I mean, I was an awfully naughty boy."

Faking a growl, I whipped off my shirt, enjoying the lust that flared in his eyes as he took in my massive chest. I schooled my face into an impassive expression and said,

"Get up and bend over my knees, boy. It's time for Daddy to show you what happens to little brats that don't behave themselves."

Ryan's eyes danced as he hopped off my lap and arranged himself across my legs. Our height difference was so drastic, that as he lay draped across me, his head and feet didn't touch the floor. Before I began, I told him, "Ryan, this is important. If it gets too intense, say peacock. I promise that word will stop me dead in my tracks. Anything else, and I'll just assume you're playing the game. Now repeat that back so that I know you're on the same page. What are you going to say if I need to stop?"

"Peacock, *Daddy*."

I ran my hand over his cheeks, rubbing and enjoying the feel of his skin. I waited for his body to relax into the massage then I lifted my hand and brought it down onto his right cheek.

SMACK!

Ryan jerked, more from the surprise than from any kind of pain. I hadn't put any force behind it, I was just warming him up. I waited again for him to settle, then brought my hand down over his left cheek.

SMACK!

He didn't move, so I built up into a steady pattern of spanking, alternating from cheek to cheek.

SMACK! SMACK! SMACK! SMACK!

His flesh began to warm up beneath my hand, turning pink. I gave a harder smack, and Ryan's hands came back to cover himself. "No, Daddy! Stop! I'll be good! No more!" His whining tone and the hardness that was pressing into my thigh told me that he was enjoying the game.

Grabbing his wrists in my non-spanking hand, I bent his elbows back and pinned his hands at the small of his back. I brought my spanking hand down hard enough then to leave a faint hand print.

SMACK!

Mesmerized, I made a matching print on the other side.

SMACK!

Encouraged by the moans that were coming from his throat and the way he was trying to find friction against my pants leg, I kept up the spanking at the new level I'd begun since he was responding to it so sweetly.

SMACK! SMACK! SMACK! SMACK!

His ass was nicely pink, and warm to the touch as I rubbed its tenderized flesh. I released his hands and grabbed him by the waist, then stood and laid him across the foot of the bed. I knelt down behind him. While I rubbed the sting from his cheeks, I couldn't resist that winking hole that was already leaking omega slick.

I ran my hands down his legs and pushed them open. Bending over him, I licked a line down his crack, then lapped at his slick hole. The sweetness of his slick coated my tongue as I eagerly licked and lapped at him before spearing my tongue right into his tight little pucker.

Ryan groaned and lifted his butt a little to grant me better access. I chuckled to myself. *Mmm, someone really likes this, huh?* My hands stroked and rubbed his cheeks in sync with my tongue that was teasing his rim. When his slick began seeping out in a steady stream, I knew that it was time to move on to the main event.

I stood and stripped off the rest of my clothes. I told Ryan, "Turn over, and scoot up to the middle of the bed for me, omega boy." He did, hissing slightly as his tender ass rubbed against the rough blanket.

Climbing onto the bed, I grabbed a soft pillow. "Lift up, baby," I said, sliding the pillow under him when he complied. I bent over and sunk my mouth down over his rigid dick, sucking him in with one move. Teasing my tongue along his silken rod, I pulled up to tease my tongue against his leaking slit. Rolling his balls in my fingers, I teased and licked at that mushroom shaped head before sucking him in again. I sucked in my cheeks, giving good suction as he began to mindlessly thrust into my mouth.

His hands grabbed at my hair, pulling it to the point of stinging. I felt his balls draw up as he gasped "Ivan," right before his nectar exploded into my mouth. I took it all, savoring every drop of his sweet essence before releasing him with a soft pop. I braced my hands beside his hips and crawled up until I covered him with my body.

Keeping the bulk of my weight on my hands and knees, I leaned in for a kiss. I pulled up, looking into his eyes. His pupils were blown wide, his cheeks flushed pink with pleasure. I touched my forehead to his and whispered against his soft lips, "Are you ready for more now, my love?"

His hand ran up my side, lightly skimming over my muscles. He nodded. "Yes, Ivan. Make me yours now. I'm ready."

I spoke gruffly, my voice choked with emotion as I replied. "I'm making you mine forever, *medvezhonok.*"

Standing on my knees, I lifted his legs. Guiding them to his chest, I looked down hungrily at his slick hole. I lined up the head of my rock hard cock with that slick pucker, and gently nudged into it. He was so ready for me that his channel practically sucked me in as I pushed slowly forward.

I watched his face closely for any sign of discomfort, but all I saw was raw need. I allowed myself to slip completely, falling forward onto my my braced hands as his legs wrapped automatically around my waist. My face level with his, I slowly began to move. His eyes fluttered open and shut and open again as I thrust slowly in and out.

Moving his hands to firmly grip my arms, Ryan spoke on a moan, "Harder, Ivan. I need to feel you."

Gritting my teeth, I began to thrust faster. I'd been worried about hurting him, but soon he was pushing back against me, meeting me thrust for thrust. I groaned as his ass began to tighten around me. The base of my cock had a strange tingling now. I lifted to one arm and bent to watch my cock plunging into that tight hole. I realized at once what the tingling was—my knot was expanding for the first time.

A wave of pleasure rolled over my body, leaving goose-bumps in its wake. I kept a steady rhythm of fast, short strokes. Slamming harder into him now, I began to thrust my hips with more abandon as Ryan writhed and screamed out my name. Sweat dripped from my face and chest, drenching my omega with every drop.

Ryan began rocking mindlessly against me, begging "Harder, Ivan! Fill me!" His flushed face and glazed eyes showed how close he was, as his tight body began to tense. His channel hugged me tight as my knot swelled hugely within his hole, trapped fast inside. Grunting, I rocked against him, chasing pleasure as my own body began to electrify and tingle with the need to fill him. To breed him. To claim him.

With one final thrust, my seed began to spill right as Ryan's dick spouted thick ropes of pearly cream. Moving quickly, I bent down and nuzzled his omega-gland.

"Ryan, claim me, baby," I managed to gasp out before sinking my already elongated teeth into his gland.

As my teeth pierced his flesh, I felt a sting over my alpha-gland as his smaller fangs sank into my skin. A wave of euphoria flooded me, and it was as if I were having an out of body experience. I had to close my eyes against the rush of blurred colors, as I rode him through the shared orgasm. I could feel myself sinking into him, but at the same time, I felt as though I were the one being sunk into. I felt the heated flood of seed filling me, and realized that I was experiencing what he was feeling.

It was magical. It was surreal. It was fucking glorious. Once the euphoria passed and I was able to open my eyes without feeling like I was floating, I licked the blood away from where I'd claimed him. My sweet little mate. My bratty omega. Mine.

I slid my arms under his back, and carefully rolled us over onto my back. I had no idea how long my knot would take to go down, and I wanted my mate comfortable in the meantime. I helped him scoot down my large body as he wriggled and adjusted himself. Once he was comfortable so that my knot wasn't tugging against his hole, we laid there peacefully for several minutes before I spoke. "That was incredible. Thank you for allowing us to give ourselves to each other, my little *medvezhonok*."

I felt his smile against my chest. "What does that word mean? I like how it sounds from your lips, but I don't know what you're saying."

"I'm calling you my teddy bear. *Medvezhonok* is teddy bear in Russian, my love."

"Wow. So you dropped the stiff, formal way of talking that your den all seems to do, but you remember your home language?"

"Yeah, pieces and snippets, I guess you'd say. So, I noticed that you never said peacock. Does that mean that you were okay with all of that?"

"Oh, hells yeah! That was hot, big boy."

"*Big boy*?" I chuckled curiously.

"Yep. I figure we can be each other's boys, since we have the right equipment." He wiggled his butt, then sucked in a sharp breath when my knot tugged against his tender rim. "Okay, I think I'll just stay still now."

"Good idea, baby. Tell me, what did you think of that crazy blending when we claimed? That was crazy, right? Nobody ever told me to expect that." I stared up at the ceiling while I threaded my fingers through his hair with one hand, and captured his hand in the other. I brought our joined hands up to my mouth and kissed his knuckles.

"I knew to expect something like that, but not nearly that intense. I mean, I've heard the other omegas talk about it, but nobody could describe that, right?"

"Yeah, I think it pretty much defies explanation." I remembered all of a sudden how his scent had smelled earlier when he'd arrived, and took a deep sniff. Yep, it was close now. "Ryan? I need to warn you of something. I'm glad we claimed now, while we both can remember our first time together."

"Why wouldn't we remember?" Ryan asked curiously.

"Because sometime within the next few hours, your body is going to go into heat. I can smell it in your pheromones. From what I've been told, you're going to be lost in a haze of lust and a blur of hungry desire until your heat passes or you are impregnated. Is that okay?"

He shrugged against me, and I could feel his lips turn up in a smile. "You bears and your crazy sniffers! I can never get over how you guys do that. But yeah, I mean, it's not like it's your fault, right? It has to be okay. I'm just glad that we got advance warning thanks to your magical nose."

I laughed. "Magical nose. Good one. But what if you get pregnant? Should we call peacock on that? Because I don't know if condoms would really work to prevent pregnancy between us."

"No, I don't mind. When I came here to accept you, I knew that would be on the table as a distinct possibility if we mated. I'm good with it, forget what I said before. I want our babies, as many as Fenris blesses us with, and having them while I'm still young enough to chase them down is good."

"Alrighty then. I know my dad is going to be excited if we

make him a Dada. And before you ask, that's a fond form of grandpa."

"I figured that, from the context of your dad. Wow, it's gonna be so awesome to be related to Doc. I love your dad so much." I could feel the happiness and peace radiating from my little omega.

"Call him Papa when you see him next, he will love it. I haven't called him that since I was a cub, and he will love to hear it from you."

"I'll do that. Wow, I've never had a dad. You should have mentioned that sooner, that might have sold me all on its own." He giggled, running an idle finger in a circle around my nipple.

"Baby, if we're ever going to get my knot down, you might want to lay off the nipple play. Just a thought."

He craned his neck back to look up at me. "What if I just get you hard instead, and ride your knot all night?"

I chuckled. "I'm going to die with you as my mate, but I think I'll go out happy." I startled all of a sudden, realizing that I had class in the morning and a newly claimed mate about to go into heat. Turning my head, I saw my phone on the nightstand. I stretched out my arm, and picked it up. After scrolling through my contacts, I found the number I wanted and fired off a text to Daniel. "Hey, baby? Your brother is about to find out about us, because I just texted Daniel to cancel school."

"Oh, hell. Okay. What did you say?"

I held out my phone so he could read it.

Claimed my mate. Cancel school for the rest of the week, he's going into heat. All is good, we'll be in touch when we are ready to see people again.

"Okay, that's fine," Ryan said as my phone pinged with an incoming text. I touched the screen and held it there so we could both read it.

Tell him Luke says congrats. Don't worry about school, the pups will be glad for a break. See you both... eventually.

Ryan snorted. "Yeah, that sounds about right. I bet Luke shit a brick. It's a good thing we already talked earlier, or he'd be the one pitching one of my famous fits."

I laughed, and put my phone aside so I could keep playing with Ryan's hair and stroking his soft skin. He yawned, and began to breathe slower. I smiled softly and let him drift off. He'd be awake and looking for a knotting soon enough when the heat came over him. It was good that he rested now. Taking my own advice, I closed my eyes and drifted off too.

Several hours later, I woke up to see Ryan straddling my hips as he sucked at my nipple. I could smell the full bloom of his heat. I grabbed him and rolled him over, nuzzling into his neck and scraping my teeth over his omega-gland. He writhed under me, whimpering with need. I lifted my head and took in his red, flushed face and glassy eyes with the blown-out pupils. His dark brown nipples were stiff enough to cut glass, while he grabbed at his painfully engorged dick.

I rolled him over onto his stomach before pulling him up onto his hands and knees as I slotted myself in behind him and sank my already hard cock right into his slick-soaked hole.

The rest of the night went by in a blur of fucking, sucking, and sweat-soaked grinding in between sessions of sleeping while Ryan was stuck on my knot. He finally fell asleep a little before dawn, and I gratefully joined him.

CHAPTER 7

RYAN

I woke up, fuzzy headed and bleary eyed. I sat up and looked over at Ivan. My poor alpha looked like he'd been ridden hard and put away wet. Oh, wait. That was pretty much exactly what I did to him. I think. It was hard to remember. I had flashes of the night before, but mostly it was just a blur of sensations.

It was good that we'd claimed before my heat hit. Now I understood what Ivan had meant by being glad that I'd actually be able to remember our first time.

"How the fuck are you sitting there looking so perky after you ravaged me all night long?"

I turned over to see Ivan looking disgruntled at being awake. I leaned over with a giggle and kissed his nose. "You stink, big boy. So do I. Do you have a shower in here?"

He looked almost insulted. "Of course I do! Do you think I don't bathe?"

I almost laughed at how what a grumpy bear he was being. I moved over and cuddled up against him, happy when a big arm wrapped immediately around my waist. I looked over at my mate. "Tell me. Are you always like this when you wake up, or is this special for me?"

He rolled his eyes and reached down to smack my butt. "Only when I've been used as a sex doll all night by my mate. So, yeah, I guess it's special for you."

He hugged me close and kissed the top of my head, making me feel like I was precious to him. "So, why are you so perky anyway? Usually I need coffee to achieve that." He yawned, and arched his back into a stretch. "You're right, though. We both need a shower. I don't even want to think about the amount of dried jizz currently covering our bodies and sheets."

I laughed then. There was something too funny about the word jizz coming out of his mouth. I got up and climbed on top of him, sitting there astraddle his hips. Catching his hands, I held them firmly while I leaned over and kissed him.

"Hi, there." I smiled as I whispered that against his lips.

"Hey, yourself," he whispered back. Then he forcefully pushed our joined hands behind my back as he leaned up to kiss me. "Okay, dirty boy. Let's go clean up. The bathroom is straight across from us, the door beside my closet." He let go of my hands and swatted my butt as I scrambled off him and scooted out of bed.

I walked into the bathroom, amazed by how roomy it was. I'd assumed that the teacher's lodging would be smaller than this was. I stopped to take a piss while Ivan came in and rifled through a drawer. He tossed an unopened toothbrush on the counter.

"Is that for me?" I asked as I flushed the toilet and moved to the sink to wash my hands.

"Yeah, unless I have another mate in here that I don't know about," he said with a smirk as he went over to the toilet to have his own turn.

"Why exactly did you have an extra toothbrush? Do I need to be jealous?" I drew myself up my full height as I looked over at him expectantly.

Ivan laughed and flushed the toilet. He came up behind me, pressing against me as he reached both hands around me to use the sink.

"I could have moved, all you had to do was ask. And speaking of asking, I believe that I asked you a question?" I was leaning against him, watching his face in the mirror while I teased him.

"Okay, jealous boy. The extra toothbrush is because they were sold in a multipack. I'd saved it for when mine wears out. Instead, I'm giving it to you. Is that okay?" He smiled patiently at me, his eyes dancing with humor.

I smiled and said, "That's a reasonable explanation. See? That wasn't so hard!"

He wiggled his brows and thrust up against me. "No, but keep sassing me like that and something else might be hard soon."

I rolled my eyes and slipped under his arm to freedom. I looked over my shoulder and winked as I went over and started the shower. I squealed as I was lifted up and carted in with him.

We had fun soaping and cleaning each other. Some parts took a little longer than others. Ivan had knelt down to carefully clean my balls, or so he claimed, when a funny look came over his face. He tilted his head and took a long inhaled sniff while pressing his ear against my stomach.

When he grinned up at me with wet eyes, I knew what he was about to say and said it for him instead. "So, my heat's definitely over, I take it? You got a hole in one on our first night out?"

Ivan threw his head back and laughed before standing and lifting me up against his chest. "Only you would make hole jokes while I'm discovering something precious."

He leaned in and kissed me gently, hugging me against him. My feet were several inches off the floor, but it felt like I was floating higher than that. Pregnant. Me! I looked into my mate's eyes and smiled. "So, I guess I have three months to learn to be a dad?"

Ivan looked scared all at once. "Three months! We have three months to find a bigger place to live, set up a nursery, not to mention all the clothes and diapers we're going to need! Oh, and I need to have Dad look you over!"

I leaned in and kissed him, silencing his stressed babble. Pulling back, I smiled into his eyes and said, "Breathe, big boy. You're supposed to be the steady, patient one. If you start freaking out like I would, our family is fucked."

He grinned. "Family. I like that. Okay, how about we wait to call Dad. Instead, I'll make us some sandwiches, change the sheets, and we can spend time snuggling instead of worrying. At least for today."

"Now that sounds like a good plan," I agreed with a smile. Alphas. They always got so weird when we omegas were pregnant.

———

After an entire week spent alone while we settled into our claim, we finally decided to go among people again. Our first stop was Luke's cabin, just to get it over with. I hadn't even made it up the walk when his door was flung open and a Luke shaped blur came flying at me.

I'm not sure how I avoided falling down, probably Ivan's steadying hand on my back. Luke hugged me so hard that it almost hurt. When he finally pulled back, he held my face in his hands as he searched my eyes.

"You're happy, brat? Really and truly?"

I sighed. "Well, you obviously know that I just spent a week getting laid. So, I'd have to say yes. I'm pretty fucking happy right about now."

Luke rolled his eyes. "Typical, Ryan. Why be serious when you can be a smartass, right?"

I narrowed my eyes. "Better a smartass than a dumbass."

We started to glare at each other in our normal go-to of posturing where we'd fight and then finally talk when we made up. Deciding to to be mature instead, I held up a hand. "Wait, Luke. I shouldn't needle you. Actually, Ivan and I are very happy. Thank you for asking. I'm sorry if I worried you."

Luke's mouth dropped open as he stared at me. Flicking a measuring gaze to Ivan before he looked back at me, Luke said, "Wow. Mating Ivan was a good idea. Apparently he's teaching you some manners. There's hope for you to grow up into an actual adult yet."

I could feel Ivan's protective irritation through our bond, but he politely smiled and said, "Actually, Luke, your brother is quite well-mannered. And I would hope that I'd mated an adult. It would be disgusting otherwise. Perhaps you two both need to do as my mate has just done and learn to be patient with each other. I realize that it must be difficult not to fall back into your childhood interactions."

Luke looked appropriately chastened, and invited us inside. I gripped Ivan's hand and looked up at him gratefully. He was right. It was difficult not to fall back into our childhood behavior when Luke and I got together. My brother was a good guy, he just wore blinders when it came to me. Hopefully with my mate's help, we might finally have an adult relationship.

When we went inside, Daniel was sitting on the couch, while the Trips crawled around the childproofed room. He grinned up at Ivan and nodded to me. "Come on in, you two. Tell us your good news so we can get busy finding you new housing."

My jaw dropped as Luke looked at me with shock. Ivan looked at Daniel curiously and asked, "And how do you know that we have good news?"

Daniel shrugged. "Past experience. We haven't had a pair of fated-mates yet that have made it out of their claiming bed without a bun in the oven."

Luke looked at Ivan, knowing full well how good the bear olfactory senses were. "And is my brother pregnant, Ivan? Am I going to be an uncle?"

Daniel and I both grinned and nodded happily. Luke hugged me again, whispering into my ear, "I'm happy for you, Ryan. I'll try to lighten up. I hope you know how much I love you. I'm sorry I'm an overbearing ass sometimes."

I hugged him back. "I love you too, Luke. We'll work it out together, okay?"

He nodded against my neck, then pulled back and grabbed my hand. Luke dragged me over to the couch and shoved me down next to where Ivan had just taken a seat. "Okay. I'm going to feed you now, and you're going to eat it without arguing."

I grinned and scooted over onto Ivan's lap. I snuggled into him, resting my head in the curve of his neck. "Okay, Luke. That actually sounds really good. This guy lives on sandwiches and fruit, so I'm pretty much starving right now."

Ivan grumbled against my ear. "You should have said something, *medvezhonok*. I would've gotten you better food."

I shrugged. "I know, but I didn't want either one of us to see people any more than you did."

Daniel smirked knowingly. "Okay. So, am I putting you guys in the cabin next door? I'm assuming that you still don't want to live in the main lodge, Ivan?"

Ivan shrugged, but I shook my head. "No, I don't think that's the best idea. What about the one next door to the schoolhouse? Then Ivan is right next door to the school, but Luke and I would have a few cabins between us. It might be safer that way."

Luke laughed from over in the kitchen area of the great room we were sitting in. "He has a point, babe. Ryan and I will get there, but living next door to each other is probably not the best plan for Ryan and me. Plus, I really don't think that either of us wants to hear the kind of noises coming from my brother's place that we sometimes hear from next door."

I looked up curiously. Luke looked over his shoulder and grinned. "Let's just say that Zane's a screamer, Karl's a moaner, and Owen? Well, let's not go there."

I laughed at the look on Daniel's face and the shudder I felt go through Ivan. "What, you two don't like to hear about your buddies getting busy?" I asked in my most innocent voice.

Daniel grinned. "I don't mind hearing about it. But actually hearing it crosses a line. That's why we're having double pane windows installed on all the cabins next month. After researching it, I decided it's cheaper than soundproofing everything and should still do the trick."

I giggled. "Maybe soundproofing their bedroom would be better. Poor Trixie and baby Carrots!"

Luke snickered. Daniel looked over at Ivan and said, "On that note, can I offer you a beer?" I giggled hard at that and snuggled into my mate. Maybe this visit with my brother and his family would be okay after all.

By the time we left a few hours later, our bellies were full and Daniel had it set up for us to move into our new cabin beside the schoolhouse the following day. Ivan led me two cabins over, and knocked on Doc's door. It was time to tell him the good news. Not that we needed to, when he took one whiff of me and beamed from ear to ear.

He smiled gently at me then and reached for a hug, ignoring his own son altogether. I remembered what Ivan had said and while he was hugging me, I said, "So now that I'm mated to your son, does that mean that I can call you Papa?"

Doc pulled me into his cabin, leaving a chuckling Ivan to follow. "Yes! Yes, you may definitely call me that, my dear boy. You are now my son's mate, which makes you my son now as well, yes?"

I nodded happily as he led me to sit at his table. He fussed around his kitchen while an amused Ivan sat down next me. Doc was humming under his breath while he pulled together a pot of tea.

As he put the pot on to heat, he looked at Ivan over his glasses. "You have made certain that our Ryan has been kept fed, yes? Lots of water? Hydration is important. Especially now that he is carrying twins."

Ivan shook his head and dropped his head onto the table. He muttered against the wooden surface, "It better not be like this for the whole pregnancy, I'm telling you that right now." His head popped up suddenly, and he leaned over to press an ear to my stomach. He sat back up and looked at me with alarm before looking at his dad. "How did I miss that second heartbeat? A cub would've heard that! I must be losing my touch." He frowned down at the table.

I smiled and reached over to rub his shoulder. Poor Ivan. It was a lot to take in. I was just rolling with it, surprisingly enough. Maybe because of the Trips? I don't know but it just didn't scare me.

I smiled as I watched Doc walking over with a cup of tea and a plate of cookies. It seemed like Doc was prepared to fuss over me now. He'd always been protective of me anyway, but now that I was carrying his grandchildren? I'm pretty sure that he was going to be amping that up to a whole new level.

We stayed and visited with Doc for about an hour, before I began to yawn. Doc assured me that it was a normal symptom of pregnancy when I commented that I shouldn't be tired this early in the evening.

After that, he gave us a list of instructions and made plans to see me in the office. As a patient though, not an employee. Before he sent us on our way, he gave stern instructions for me not to be seen at work. Apparently, I was about to be out of a job and Doc would have to start fresh with another assistant. Oh, well. Not my problem. I just wanted to go home and sleep for a week or two. Three at the most.

CHAPTER 8

IVAN

The new cabin was finally coming together, I thought as I stood looking around at the new double pane windows that had been installed. Ryan came wandering in and stood in the doorway looking at me.

I'd just finished putting together the second crib. Every day this week, I'd come home after work and spent an hour or two in the nursery. I'd painted the walls a bright happy yellow color, and now I was putting together the white furniture set that Ryan had picked out for our children.

Now that he was heading into his third month, we knew that we were having fraternal twins. Our family would be truly mixed. Our son was definitely a wolf, while our daughter was a bear. The pack was astounded by this, but Dad simply shrugged and gave a lecture on genetics to anyone that asked.

"Are you about done here for the day, big boy? I've got dinner ready." Ryan had a knowing smile on his face as he stood there with a hand resting on his big bump. I stood and stretched before I walked over to pull him up against me for a kiss.

"Sorry, baby. Did I take too long again?" I had a tendency to lose time while I was daydreaming in the nursery.

"No, not really. But we have the pack meeting tonight, so I figured that we'd eat early," Ryan explained with a smile as we took our seats at the table. Ryan began to fill our plates with salad and pasta.

I looked with interest at the food, as I rolled my eyes about the pack meeting. That meant that we'd be out late, and I had an early morning at the schoolhouse. Not to mention the fact that Ryan was always tired. He'd had an easy pregnancy so far, with no morning sickness or other common complaints. Except that he was always tired. He'd wake up, and be ready to take a nap an hour later. The fact that Dad denied him coffee didn't help matters.

"Do you remember what this meeting is about? I forget," Ryan said with a pout. That was the other thing. The poor guy couldn't remember for shit. It really pissed him off, too. The other omegas just glared at him when he complained and told him to come back when he was puking up his intestines and had ankles swollen like grapefruit.

"Mikael, the Alpha from the den, has asked to speak with

our pack. I think that he has something planned with Jake, to be honest. But I don't know." I shrugged. "Still, I guess it will be nice to see Mikael. He's always been a friend."

"Did you guys grow up together?" Ryan asked curiously, as he took a bite of the lasagna he'd made for us.

I laughed. "No, Mikael is five years older than me. But we lived next door to each other before his father passed and he became Alpha. That was about the same time that I left for college."

Ryan swallowed a bite of salad before asking, "Did you also know his sister that he had shunned? And what's up with the whole shunning thing? Is that really a permanent thing?"

I explained as well as I could. "I knew Yvonne, yes, but I avoided her. She was always a crazy bitch. And yes, shunning is definitely a thing. And it is a permanent thing. There is no coming back from a shunning, but they are only used for the worst crimes. And honestly, if a person is that evil, why would we want them back in our den?"

Ryan nodded. "Yeah, but shunning them makes them someone else's problem. You have to admit that there's something not right about that."

"True. Would you have had us kill the bad apples instead? We bears aren't as bloodthirsty as one would think. We are actually a peaceful people."

Ryan shrugged. "I don't know. And I suppose this conversation has probably gotten too deep for dinner. I'm thinking now about back when Jake killed Alpha Fremont. If we'd just shunned him, he would've just kept kidnapping or buying omegas to imprison and force to breed heirs for him. I just think we need a better system. Maybe prisons with silver bars? I don't know. Something. I just don't like to think of evil people roaming free."

I smiled at my normally peaceful little mate as I stood and cleared the table. "You make a good point, my love. But I don't think we shifters can do something like that without the humans eventually catching on. It's a tough one."

We continued our conversation as we dressed for the meeting and walked over to the lodge. I enjoyed Ryan's intelligence and wit. He'd been afraid that I'd find him too young and immature at first, yet he was my equal and we'd shared many wonderful conversations already in our time together. I smiled, and put my arm around him. I was thinking of the years stretching ahead of us into the future and all the conversations that we'd share along the way.

Ryan and I took our seats that the peacock had saved next to his own. I had begrudgingly began to finally accept their friendship now that we were officially mated. I could feel Ryan's complete lack of attraction for the other omega, which helped a lot in making me relax where he was concerned.

When Mikael and Jake stepped up to the front of the room, the peacock paled and swayed in his seat. I looked at him with alarm. I nudged Ryan, and tipped a chin toward his friend. They exchanged a whispered conversation, then fell silent. I shrugged. Ryan would tell me later. Or he wouldn't. It was not of much matter to me, as long as the kid was okay.

When Jake and Mikael announced a joint cooperative between our two communities, the peacock sat up and paid more attention. Mikael was explaining. "We have seen how well some of our own people have integrated here, and would like to offer the same possibility for any interested wolves to come work among us or even stay at the den."

Jake added, "The bears haven't been as lucky finding mates in the recent years. What Mikael is too polite to say is that he's offering for our single pack members to interact with his single den members in the hopes of more fated-mate pairings being discovered. We will be hosting a rotating group of bears, and Mikael will do the same. We figure a month is a good time period for the exchange members to stay in the opposite community."

Mikael picked up the thread of conversation and explained further. "Nobody will be required to do this, it is simply an option that we wish to offer to interested parties. Our guests will stay in my home, and be welcome to move around our town to meet our residents. We will host two of you, starting next month. And in turn, two of our eligible single bears will come here. You will each stay for a month, and return home if you haven't found a mate. Are there any questions?"

Of course my Ryan had a question. "And what if they do find mates? Where will they live? In the alpha's home community?" Every omega in the room sat up and waited for the answer to that one.

Mikael smiled easily. "No, not at all. And by the way," he stopped and winked at me, "allow me to pause to congratulate you and my friend, Ivan. Both on your mating, and for your twins."

Mikael turned his attention back to the meeting and continued. "What Jake and I have discussed is that we will leave that up to each individual couple. No one will know better than the parties themselves what will work best for them."

Jake added, "Mikael and I have agreed that we'd rather lose members of our communities than to see our friends lose out on finding a fated-mate."

The meeting wound down after that. Peacock ducked away as Mikael made his way over to us. He greeted me with a big hug. "Ivan, how are you? It is good to see you, and to see you happily settled."

I grinned and proudly introduced Ryan to Mikael. Mikael asked with just a little too much interest about

Ryan's little blue-haired friend. Ryan prattled on about his friend, Taylor. As soon as Mikael learned that the peacock was a single omega, I noted a flash of intrigue in his eyes. Unless I was imagining it. Who knows.

As we walked home with Luke and Daniel, the brothers were chattering about the new plan and what it might mean for the future of our communities. Daniel and I talked about babies, and he offered to send me links he'd saved from when their pups were born about caring for multiples.

After we got inside and settled into bed, Ryan yawned before pointing out how funny it was that the omegas were the ones discussing community concerns while the two alphas had been talking babies. I grinned and pulled the little brat into my arms. Yeah, the stereotypes definitely did not fit the omegas of this pack, but especially my mate. If I'd ever thought I'd be mated to a sweet, submissive omega that would do what I wanted and follow my directions, I'd been sorely mistaken. My sassy little mate was proud to say that he was not a typical little omega bitch. Even if he was a little brat, he was all mine.

The pregnancy had flown by, and I was days away from delivering. Taylor came over every day now, and stayed with me until Ivan came home again. Nobody wanted me alone with twins on the way, so Taylor was excused from duties and sent to babysit me. He couldn't be happier about it either.

"So what do you think, Ry? Should I do it? I mean, I could break free and finally have a chance at a little freedom. But on the other hand, the bears are a bit stiff. What if I don't fit in over there?"

I reached over and grabbed his hand, pulling him down onto the couch next to me. "Dude. Calm your shit. You and I both know that you're totally going for it, so just let go of your worries, and give it a shot. Besides, they'll be more worried about whether you're somebody's fated-mate than about the color of your hair."

Taylor grinned. "Not to mention, I'd get to stay with that hot as hell Alpha. Did you see him? Holy shit!"

I nodded. "Yeah, Mikael is so huge that he makes the other bears look small. And that's saying a lot! You know Oskar? The bear omega? He got injured, and Mikael straight up lifted and carried him like he was our size!"

Taylor's eyes grew wide. "Wow. Can you imagine how strong he must be then?"

I looked at my friend with narrowed eyes. "Are you going over there just to get closer to Mikael?"

Taylor shrugged. "I mean, I'm not going to avoid him. But I dunno. There was something about him that intrigued me."

I shook my head with a grin. "Yeah, you just want to know if the penis size is proportional to the rest of his body."

With a shout of laughter, Taylor threw his head back. He looked over at me and shook his head. "You're getting to be worse than I am. But seriously, Ry! I only need to see him shift once and I'll have my answer."

I punched his shoulder, shaking with giggles. The rest of our day flew by, until Ivan finally made it home from school. Or so I liked to tease him. Taylor leaned in and kissed my cheek. "Don't drop any babies tonight, and I'll see you tomorrow, m'kay?"

He sauntered out the door while Ivan grabbed a couple of

waters and came over to sit beside me on the couch. He held out his arms and pulled me onto his lap.

"How's my main guy today? Are the babies kicking a lot?" He nuzzled over my claim-bite and kissed his mark.

I shuddered and told him about my boring day and Taylor's plans to try to see the mighty Alpha cock of Mikael. Ivan cracked up at that one. "Good luck to Taylor. I don't think that Mikael is going to be so wound up by the little peacock that he willingly allows him to creep on him like that."

With a shrug, I said, "You never know. Look at us. We aren't exactly a couple that people would've put together."

Ivan grunted out a laugh. "If that little peacock ends up with any bear in that den, let alone the Alpha, I'm gonna laugh my ass off. Baby, you don't understand! The bears are a quiet community of reserved country folk. Taylor will scare the life out of them!"

I smiled. "Or breathe the life back into them. Either way, he's only leaving for a month, what's the worst that could happen?"

Ivan agreed. His lips moved up my neck to nibble at my ear. "Why are we talking about the peacock anyway? I've got my lap full of my sexy mate. Who, I must say, has far too many clothes on for my taste."

I shuddered as he bit my earlobe. "You're welcome to undress me."

No sooner than the words were out of my mouth, Ivan was in motion. He lifted me easily so that I was standing in front of him, and yanked my pants down to my ankles. I held his shoulder while he helped me step out of them.

Laughing, I looked at his tented crotch with a raised brow. He grinned up at me with an apologetic wince. "I may have jumped a few steps ahead of you already."

I smirked at him, well aware of how turned on he was by my pregnancy. I don't know why, but the larger I got, the more he was just constantly hard. I teased that it was because he knew that he'd bred two babies into me and he got turned on by his own handiwork. He didn't deny it, that's all I'm saying.

"Okay, but I'm tired, so I'm all about a quickie. Yank that bad boy out and let me sit on it." Ivan looked at me in surprise, but I was totally serious. "I mean it. Come on, big boy. I'd stroke my dick right now, but I can't find it anymore."

Ivan laughed and reached out to give me a quick tug. "There he is, alive and well."

"Yeah, well, he might as well be missing in action for all I know. Now hurry up, I wanna take a nap on your knot." Ivan grinned at my bossy tone, and pushed his pants down, kicking them to the side. "Guide me down, big boy, I want to go back to chest so we can spoon after."

"Bossy brat today, huh?" He ran a finger down my crack, fingering my hole to make sure I was slick enough. I already knew I was. I'd been thinking about fucking him since lunchtime, I just didn't want to admit it to him. He found out soon enough.

"Mmhmm. Looks like somebody was already on board, you little brat. Get over here and sit on my cock." He threw his stern alpha voice into the command, making me shiver with anticipation.

Grabbing my hips, Ivan guided me down onto his lap. He expertly lined up his cock with one hand and eased it into me as I slowly lowered myself onto it with his helpful hand stabilizing my hip.

I sank down onto his fat cock with a lusty moan. "Fuck, yeah! That's what I needed, big boy!" My head lolled back onto his shoulder, my hand reached behind for his hips. I rocked against him with a firm hold on his hips for support.

Ivan's large hands roamed my torso while he thrust rhythmically up into my body. He cupped my mound of baby belly with one hand, while the other pinched at my nipples one at at time. I brought my hands up to play with my nipples and grunted, "I need that hand further south."

With a soft chuckle, Ivan reached a hand under my belly to stroke my swollen dick. He kissed and nuzzled my ear. Moving his lips along my neck and across my omega-gland before moving back up my neck and going back to suck at my ear.

I ground my ass against him, desperately seeking relief. With a tight grip on my cock, Ivan thrust up with hard, fast jerk. I gasped and pinched my nipples. Turning my head, I licked the sweat from his neck and nibbled along his jaw as he sped up. Hips pumping up faster, he thrust up hard and fast while I ground back against him.

Finally, I felt his knot begin to swell. As soon as his glorious knot swelled up against that magical little bundle of nerves, my vision blurred and I began frantically rocking my hips.

I felt heat fill my channel as Ivan shot his load up inside me. Ivan ran his thumb over the head of my dick, and stroked me with a firm twist of his wrist. When I began to shoot, he moved his thumb and let it fly. I opened my eyes to see spurts of cum shoot out in an arc and land on the coffee table and on my knees. I'm pretty sure that I even felt a fat glop land on my foot.

As soon as my breathing returned to normal, I giggled against Ivan's ear. "Did you see that cumshot? That was impressive."

Ivan snorted. "I'd ask where you picked that phrase up, but I know who you hang out with every day."

I shrugged. Again, he wasn't wrong. I grinned and said sleepily, "You know me so well. Now help us lay down on the couch, please. I need that nap. And don't roll your eyes at me, I can practically hear you doing it."

Ivan chuckled and lowered us sideways onto the couch. Luckily, it was a nice deep couch so that there was plenty of room for my large bear of a man and his big bellied mate. Ivan spoke against my ear. "I love how you think you know me, brat."

"I do know you, big boy. And your penchant for eye-rolling. You're worse than me now. But, I love you." I smiled sleepily as his hand rested protectively over my belly.

"I know you too, brat. Don't forget that. I love you and everything about you." He kissed the nape of my neck as he spoke.

I was drifting off to sleep as I mumbled, "You just want me for my body and my smart mouth, admit it." I fell asleep to the sound of his laughter.

━━

I woke up a few hours later, drenched in sweat and covered in piss. "Ivan, help me. I think I pissed myself," I was ready to cry with embarrassment. Ivan sat up and sniffed the air as he looked down at me. "No, you didn't."

I started to turn to look at him when I was bent double with by sharp cramp across my abdomen. It was as if my insides were being pulled, twisted, and tied in a knot all at once. "Fuck!" I screamed as I panted for air.

"You're in labor, baby. I'm going to ease my way up and leave you here while I call my dad." He quickly scooted out from behind me and rooted through his pants for his phone. He tapped out a quick text to his dad as I screamed loudly when another pain hit me.

His phone rang, and he actually fucking answered it while I panted and screamed in the background. I listened to his conversation, and desperately tried to get his attention because it felt like something was wedged between my legs.

I pushed back up on the couch, so that I could sit up a little. Sweat was pouring off my face as I gritted my teeth and obeyed my body's biological demand to push.

"I can't leave him, Dad." I hissed in pain and bore down while he paused to listen.

"Yes. I know all about your fucking no alphas in the delivery room rule." I gasped his name, and the idiot held up a palm to ask me to wait! Oh, fuck, I was gonna kill him! But first, I needed to push.

"No, I'll leave when you get here. I've seen labors before, and he's actually ready to deliver, I would swear to it. I'm not leaving him alone right now." He paused to listen, while I grabbed the remote from the coffee table and finally threw it at his head to get his attention.

His head jerked around in shock but when his eyes looked down between my legs, they bugged out and he hurriedly said into the phone, "Forget ready to deliver, I'm looking at a fucking head! Get over here!"

Throwing down the phone, he came over and guided me into a better position. He got between my legs and looked up at me. "I can't believe you got this far on your own. I'm so sorry! Just push through the next contraction, and I'll pull the baby out."

I panted at him, furious as fuck that this was happening like this. "Are you sure you won't have to take a call?"

He winced but before he could say anything, the next contraction hit and I bore down again. The front door flew open and Doc came flying in with Luke on his heels right as Ivan delivered our first child.

I would've laughed at the look on Doc and my brother's faces if I hadn't been in so much fucking pain. Ivan expertly stood while holding the slippery, muck-covered baby as his dad took his place. Luke stepped up with Doc's bag, and fiddled around in there while Doc firmly directed me to keep pushing.

Luke found what he was looking for, and I noticed him cutting the cord while I screamed through another contraction. Ivan darted off with the baby, while I cussed him out. I was halfway through the story of how I'd been pushing out a baby while he took a fucking phone call when Doc looked up at me with a patient smile.

He was holding the other baby in his hands. I stopped talking as tears of relief flowed down my face. Luke cut the second baby's cord, and held it up to show me. "It's your boy, Ryan." He smiled happily, his eyes filled with tears.

Doc was massaging my belly and instructing me to push again. I distractedly did as he instructed, while I watched Luke walk away with my son. Ivan came back in, carrying our daughter. She'd been cleaned up, and was wrapped in a little pink blanket when he came over and laid her in my arms.

He helped me hold her as my body wracked with sobs. Ivan bent over and softly kissed my forehead. "I'm so sorry I took that phone call, *medvezhonok*. I had no idea that you were that close to delivery."

I wanted to cuss at him some more, but I wanted to hold my baby more. And my other baby. And let my stupid mate hold me. I glared at him reproachfully.

"I'll forgive you this time. But if I ever go through this again? I will cut you if you take a call."

Ivan laughed through his tears and agreed. "It's a deal, *medvezhonok*."

I noticed Doc smiling affectionately at his son, and looked at him curiously. Doc was busy cleaning me up and dealing with the aftermath of the birth but looked up and explained, "It is good to hear my son using his Russian words. It warms an old man's heart to see his son carrying our traditions on, yes?"

Ivan leaned over and kissed our little girl before responding. "It feels right, Papa. It's good to share our culture with my mate."

Doc's glasses fogged a little at Ivan's words, but he kept going as he diligently finished up with me. Luke came over and handed our son to Ivan. He pitched in and helped Doc clear everything away so that we could all enjoy the babies.

With Doc and Luke each holding a baby, Ivan stood and lifted me from the couch. I realized with a start as he carried me into the shower to help me clean up that he had also been naked this whole time. I began to laugh my ass off, giggling almost hysterically the whole time that Ivan cleaned us both.

He patted me dry with a fresh towel before carrying me back to our room. After he helped me into a loose pair of boxers and an over-sized t-shirt, Ivan helped me into bed. He pulled on a pair of sweats and leaned out the door to call our family in.

Luke came in and climbed up on the bed beside me before passing my son into my arms. Doc reluctantly gave our daughter to Ivan, who came and sat beside me. Ivan looked up with a smile. "Okay, you guys have waited long enough. Dada? Uncle Luke? Meet Anna and Otto."

Doc's eyes teared up when he heard the names, and he

fumbled for a seat at the foot of the bed. Luke looked at him curiously as I explained.

"Anna is named for Ivan's mother, while Otto is named for Doc's father. We wanted to use family names, but ours isn't full of names worth remembering. So we decided to honor Ivan's side."

Luke nodded with a soft smile, and went around to give Doc a hug. Luke looked over at me as he went over to admire Anna again. "That's beautiful, Ryan. I love that you guys did that. It's good that your little ones will have a family heritage to be proud of, you know?"

I nodded in full agreement. My babies would have the stable home and family history that my brother and I had been cheated of having. I smiled down at my pup, happy that he would never know the pain that my brother and I had known. Glancing over at our cub in Ivan's arms, I was struck all over again with the same happy certainty of the secure childhood in her future.

CHAPTER 10

IVAN

The pack party was in full swing when Ryan and I walked in carrying our babes. Almost immediately, a swarm of our friends crowded around to lay eyes on the miracle twins that Ryan had delivered almost single-handedly.

My Papa was proudly telling anyone who would listen that his grandchildren were both already lifting their heads and looking around at only a week old. I rolled my eyes and let him brag.

Karl stepped up beside me, leaning in with Owen at his side while their mate, Zane, stood by Ryan. They all admired our pup and our cub. Zane asked for a retelling of the now famous birth story. Daniel caught my eye with a grin as Ryan bragged about dinging me upside the head with that damned remote while a baby was sticking out of his body and I was busy on the phone oblivious to the whole thing.

Karl laughed and said: "Perhaps this is why Doc Ollie does not allow the alpha fathers in during the delivery, yes? We are too easily distracted?"

Everyone laughed and Daniel spoke over Owen's shoulder. "I told him that he didn't know what he was in for if he mated Luke's kid brother. And look, the brat almost killed him with a remote over a simple phone call. Maybe it was an important call!" He laughed as he teased me.

Kai shoved his way through to get to the babies, with Aries and Sy right behind him. "Well, from what I've heard, it kinda was an important call because he was talking to Doc about the delivery. But my advice?" He looked up at me with an impish grin. "Next time, just put it on speaker and pay attention to your damn mate!"

Aunt Kat came bustling up with Jake. She squeezed Ryan's waist and whispered loudly, "You did good, son. These babies are gorgeous. Now if you have a hard time getting back on the horse, or knot as it were, come see me. I have some edible body lotions that heat and tingle! You won't even know what hit you!"

Jake gently eased his aunt towards the refreshment table, with a wink to us over his shoulder. Ryan was giggling, though. The other omegas had made off with our babies, so I scooped up my little brat and carried him over to sit by Maxx and Oskar. Maxx held their baby, Hope, on his lap.

Oskar smiled happily when he saw me, jumping up to

give me a big hug. Ryan and I spent time catching up
with them while our pack fought over who got to hold our
twins. I was amused to see my Papa walk over to Kai and
silently hold out his hands for the cub. Kai quickly passed
Anna into her Dada's capable hands, and he walked off
with his prize, cooing at her over the rim of his glasses.

Seth came over and kissed Ryan on the top of his head,
before reaching out to shake my hand. Turning back to
Ryan, Seth said, "You know, I'm realizing as I look around
the room that we've finally come full circle. You're the last
of the rescued omegas to be mated, finally putting an end
to that chapter in our pack's history."

Sy walked over and wrapped his arm around his mate's
waist. "Seth gets heavy sometimes, don't mind him," he
said to me by way of apology.

Ryan spoke up, though. "No, Seth is right. That chapter
is closed now. Look around. Our pack is filled with loving
fated-mates, and children of all ages. We all made it
through that experience, and came out the other side
happy and whole. If Alpha Jake and the guys hadn't
rescued us, who knows where we would've ended up?
Instead of a bad ending, we all got to have our happily
ever afters instead."

Luke walked over and sat down beside his brother, wrap-
ping his arms around him. "I'm just glad that our happily
ever afters included us all still being here together, in a
pack filled with old friends and new."

Speaking of new, I noticed Taylor slipping up behind Ryan. He leaned over my mate's shoulder and said, "I thought I told you not to drop those babies without me there? It figures though. With your reputation as the pack brat? You probably threw a fit and they both fell right out, huh?"

Ryan grinned and said, "Actually? You're not that far off. Sit down and let me tell you what really happened, you're gonna die!" I groaned and looked up at the ceiling as Ryan giggled and began to tell his birthing story, once again, of me talking on the phone while he pushed out our daughter. When he hit the part with the remote, everyone listening was roaring with laughter.

I looked over at my mate fondly, happy to hear him tell his story. After all, he'd earned the right to tell it as many times as he wanted after what he'd gone through. I looked around at this crazy pack that had somehow built themselves up from a tragic beginning and managed to form a large family together.

And now my Papa and I were part of that family, along with Karl and Oskar. I wondered how many bears or even other shifters might join this wacky group of people and how many wolves might go to shake things up in the bear den.

I couldn't help but smile. No matter what the future held for this wonderful community of shifters, I knew that I would be along for the ride. With my bratty little mate and our precious twins at my side.

fin

What happens when your fated mate is also your natural predator?

Join my mailing list and get your FREE copy of The Rabbit Chase:

https://dl.bookfunnel.com/vfk1sa9pu3

Twitter:
https://twitter.com/SusiHawkeAuthor

Facebook:
https://www.facebook.com/SusiHawkeAuthor

Northern Lodge Pack Series

Omega Stolen: Book 1

Omega Remembered: Book 2

Omega Healed: Book 3

Omega Shared: Book 4

Omega Matured: Book 5

Omega Accepted: Book 6

Omega Grown: Book 7

Northern Pines Den Series

Alpha's Heart: Book 1

Alpha's Mates: Book 2

Alpha's Strength: Book 3

Alpha's Wolf: Book 4

Alpha's Redemption: Book 5

Alpha's Solstice: Book 6

Blood Legacy Chronicles

Alpha's Dream: Book 1

Non-Shifter Contemporary Mpreg

Pumpkin Spiced Omega: The Hollydale Omegas - Book 1

Cinnamon Spiced Omega: The Hollydale Omegas - Book 2

Peppermint Spiced Omega: The Hollydale Omegas - Book 3

Made in the USA
Las Vegas, NV
27 March 2022

46372160R00083